LIFETIME PASSES

TERRY BLAS
CLAUDIA AGUIRRE

Abrams ComicArts SURELY, New York

VALLEY CARE LIVING.

JACKIE, I NEED YOUR HELP FOR A MINUTE. CARRIE'S ON HER BREAK.
OH, SURE, TÍA GINA.
WE NEED TO PACK UP ALL OF THESE THINGS AND GET THEM TO STORAGE SO THE FAMILY CAN COME PICK THEM UP.
THEY ASKED US TO TAKE CARE OF THIS BECAUSE THEY CAN'T MAKE IT DOWN UNTIL TOMORROW. PLUS, WE NEED THE ROOM FOR ANOTHER RESIDENT.
THIS IS . . . A LOT OF BOOKS.
AND PLANTS.
AND PILLOWS.
OH! THIS WAS THAT MEAN WOMAN WHO ALWAYS WORE THE PINK ROBE AND SLIPPERS.

KEEP IT DOWN, JACKIE. DON'T SPEAK ILL OF THE DEAD.
HER NAME WAS TRUDY, AND SHE WASN'T MEAN.

WELL SHE WASN'T **NICE.** LOOKS LIKE SHE PROBABLY HAD MORE BOOKS THAN VISITORS.
CAN'T WE JUST TOSS A BUNCH OF THIS JUNK?
THAT'S NOT NICE.

BUT IF HER FAMILY DOESN'T WANT HER BOOKS, WE COULD INCLUDE THEM IN OUR SMALL LIBRARY. WE'LL HAVE TO WAIT AND SEE.

GO GRAB ME THE DUSTER FROM YOUR CART, WILL YOU?

COUGH
COUGH

GOOD DAY, PHYLLIS.

YOU COULDN'T POSSIBLY KNOW THAT YET, ALLEN.

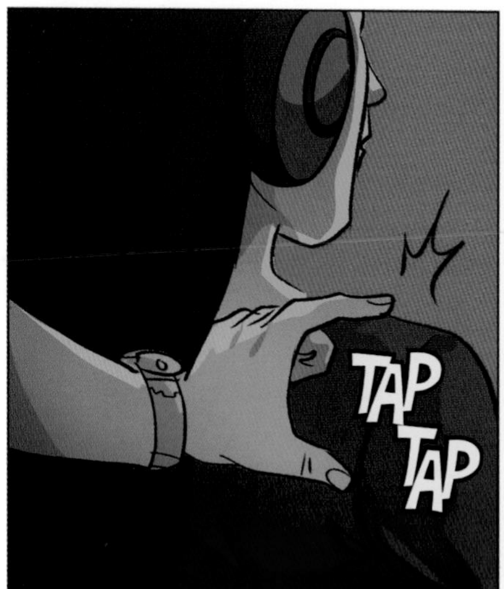
TAP
TAP

OH, THE DUSTER— HERE.
MEXICANA

GETTING A LITTLE SIDE-TRACKED?

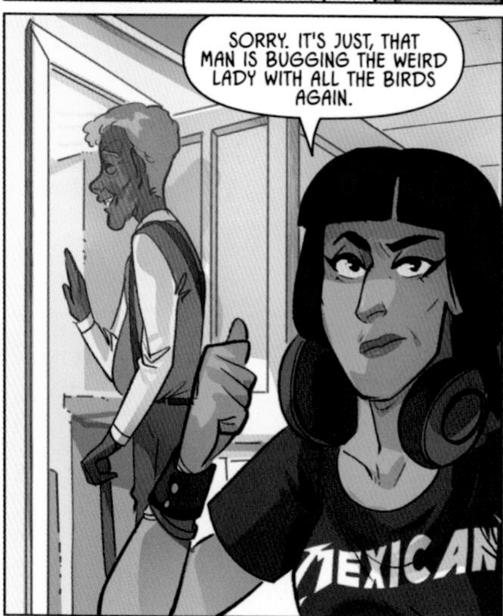
SORRY. IT'S JUST, THAT MAN IS BUGGING THE WEIRD LADY WITH ALL THE BIRDS AGAIN.
MEXICAN

MRS. ADLER? EVERYTHING ALL RIGHT?
DING DING!
YES, DEAR. ALLEN WAS JUST LEAVING ME TO MY STORIES.

HAVE A NICE DAY, MR. JONES. YOU TOO, MRS. ADLER.
THANK YOU, DARLING.
ONE DAY, PHYLLIS. I DON'T GOT TOO MANY LEFT, YOU KNOW.

YOU'RE JUST ABOUT DONE, AREN'T YOU? YOU CAN GO.
I APPRECIATE THE HELP, BUT I WANT YOU TO DO SOMETHING WITH YOUR SUMMER.
WHAT DO YOU CALL *THIS*?

SOMETHING IN THE SUNSHINE, JACKIE. I . . . I'M SORRY I CAN'T TAKE MORE TIME OFF OR TAKE US ON A TRIP OR SOMETHING–
IT'S OKAY, TÍA. REALLY.

GO SEE YOUR FRIENDS. YOUR PHONE'S BEEN GOING OFF ALL DAY.
THEY OBVIOUSLY WANT TO SEE YOU.
DING DING!

Valencia
City of Santa Clarita
DING DING!

OMG COME OVER RIGHT NOW.

OMG COME OVER RIGHT NOW.
Where are you?! 911! It's important!
UGH, you're the worst. Get over here!

I'm here.

Finally. Took you long enough.

CALM DOWN, NIKKI. I WAS HELPING MY AUNT.
WELL NOW THAT WE ARE ALL HERE, WE CAN FINALLY GET INTO IT.
BERKE! CAN YOU STOP MESSING WITH YOUR CHANNEL FOR A FEW MINUTES PLEASE?
IF YOU'RE GONNA TALK, THEN TALK. I GUARANTEE WHAT I'M DOING IS MORE IMPORTANT.
CLICK CLACK CLACK
DON'T THINK YOU CAN BE RUDE JUST BECAUSE. YOU'RE MY COUSIN. THAT'S SUPPOSED TO BEMORE LIKE A FRIEND THAN A RUDE BROTHER.
WHAT YOU BOTH ARE DOING IS VALID AND IMPORTANT. BUT I'M SURE THIS WON'T TAKE LONG, AND ONCE NIKKI'S DONE, YOU CAN GO BACK TO WHAT YOU'RE DOING.
FINE.
CAN WE GET ON WITH IT, PLEASE?

SO NONE OF YOU HAVE HEARD THE NEWS?
WHAT NEWS?

I READ ABOUT IT ALREADY THIS MORNING. IT'S STILL TRENDING.

WHAT HAPPENED?

WELL, THIS MORNING IT WAS ANNOUNCED THAT KINGDOM ADVENTURE IS BEING MADE INTO A MAJOR LIVE-ACTION STUDIO FEATURE FILM!

OH MY GOD, REALLY? THAT'S SO COOL!
YEAH, I'M OVERCOME WITH EMOTION.
WHAT ARE YOU TALKING ABOUT?

THERE ALREADY IS A KINGDOM ADVENTURE MOVIE. THE ONE FROM, LIKE, 1986.
DUH. I KNOW THAT.

BUT IT WAS REPORTED THIS MORNING THAT A **NEW** LIVE-ACTION FEATURE FILM REBOOTING THE WHOLE KINGDOM IS GOING TO BE MADE, AND THEY'RE STARTING PRE-PRODUCTION NOW!

NO. WAY. SERIOUSLY?

I CAN'T WAIT! JUST IMAGINE ALL THE NEW KINGDOM ADVENTURE MOVIE MERCH!
I HAVE TO START SAVING NOW!
THIS IS AMAZING!
I'M DYING! I'M DYING!

I FEEL LIKE IT'S ALL HAPPENING! EVER SINCE I WAS LITTLE, PLAYING PRINCESS BRIANNA AT THE PARK IS ALL I'VE EVER WANTED.
YOU KNOW THAT. I'D BE SO PERFECT FOR IT.

YOU **SO** WOULD! I'M AUDITIONING FOR PRINCE CYRIC WITH YOU! I DO HAVE THE RIGHT LOOK FOR IT.

I UNDERSTAND BERKE'S LACK OF EXCITEMENT, BUT WHAT IS **YOUR** PROBLEM, JACKIE?

NO, I'M EXCITED . . . JUST . . . WOW.
COOL. WELL, I THINK A CELEBRATORY TRIP IS IN ORDER. LET'S KICK OFF THE SUMMER RIGHT AND GO TO THE PARK TOMORROW!
I'M DOWN.

I DON'T HAVE ANYTHING BETTER TO DO NOW THAT MY YOUVID CHANNEL IS SUSPENDED.
SUSPENDED? WHY?

IT'S SO STUPID. I WAS FILMING THIS VIDEO AND DRINKING BEAST, AND I POURED ONE OUT FOR SOME RANDO WHOSE GRAVE I WAS STANDING OVER AND PEOPLE ONLINE STARTED SAYING I WAS DISRESPECTING THE DEAD.
HOW IS POURING ONE OUT DISRESPECTING THE DEAD? THAT'S, LIKE, ***HONORING*** THE DEAD, DUDE.

MAYBE CAUSE IT'S AN ENERGY DRINK?
WHATEVER.

SNOWFLAKES ALL OVER SOCIAL MEDIA WERE TRYING TO CANCEL ME. I LOST SUBSCRIBERS. *BEAST* THREATENED TO PULL THEIR SPONSORSHIP, SO I NEED TO REBRAND MY CHANNEL. IF MY VIDEOS AREN'T MONETIZED ANYMORE, I'M SCREWED.
IT'S THE ONLY WAY I MAKE MONEY, MAN.

WELL, THIS IS PERFECT, THEN. THE PARK WILL BE A NICE DISTRACTION FROM THE HATERS.
GIVE YOU A CHANCE TO CLEAR YOUR MIND.

UH . . . THERE'S A SLIGHT PROBLEM.

GO ON.

MY PARENTS ARE OUT OF TOWN THIS WEEKEND.
I HAVE TO WATCH MY LITTLE BROTHER.

FIGURE IT OUT. GET A SITTER. DO WHAT YOU HAVE TO. NOTHING IS KEEPING US FROM KINGDOM ADVENTURE TOMORROW.

NOTHING!

MEXICANA
JACKIE?
JACKIE! YOUR HEADPHONES!

WHAT? OH, SORRY.
IT'S OKAY. HOW WAS YOUR DAY? DID YOU SEE YOUR FRIENDS?
YEAH, I DID.

I HEARD ABOUT THE KINGDOM ADVENTURE MOVIE. THAT'S EXCITING.
YEAH, IT'S REALLY COOL.

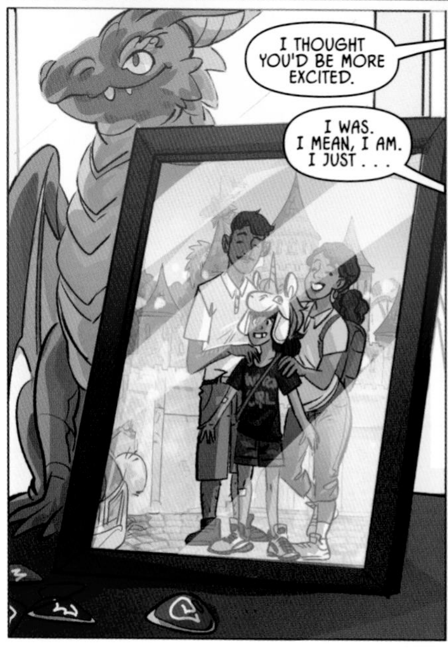
I THOUGHT YOU'D BE MORE EXCITED.
I WAS. I MEAN, I AM. I JUST . . .

I JUST WISH MOM AND DAD WERE HERE.
I KNOW, MI AMOR.
I KNOW.

MY FRIENDS WANT TO GO TO THE PARK TOMORROW TO CELEBRATE. IS THAT OKAY?
OF COURSE.

YOU DID SAY YOU WANT ME TO GET OUT THIS SUMMER.
MEXICAN

THIS PROBABLY ISN'T THE BEST TIME TO BRING IT UP, AMOR, BUT YOUR SEASON PASS? FOR THE PARK . . .

I CAN'T AFFORD TO RENEW IT AFTER THE SUMMER. IT'S REALLY EXPENSIVE, AND I'VE HAD TO TAKE MORE HOURS AT VALLEY CARE JUST TO PAY SOME BILLS. I'M REALLY SORRY, JACKIE.

BUT, I . . . I'VE ALWAYS HAD A PASS. HOW AM I SUPPOSED TO GO?
YOU MIGHT NOT BE ABLE TO FOR A WHILE.
XICAN

I KNOW HOW MUCH IT MEANS TO YOU. I'M SORRY, BUT RIGHT NOW I CAN'T PROMISE YOU ANYTHING.
IT'S ALL RIGHT. MAYBE . . . WE CAN FIND ANOTHER WAY.
MAYBE. DINNER IN AN HOUR. COME HELP ME SET THE TABLE IN A LITTLE BIT?
YES, TÍA.

KINGDOM ADVENTURE.

COME ON, GUYS. HURRY UP!

I'VE GOT ENOUGH WATER AND SNACKS TO LAST US SEVERAL HOURS, SO WE ARE GOOD TO GO.
COME ON, YOU GUYS.

COME ON, CALEB, KEEP UP.
WHY ARE WE IN A HURRY?
IS THAT BERKE BRIDGETOWER OVER THERE?
IN THE HAT?

LET'S GO.

STAY CLOSE, CALEB. PUT YOUR TABLET AWAY.
KNOCK IT OFF, DANNY. JUST LET ME READ.

THIS IS RIDICULOUS.
I TOLD YOU TO GET A SITTER. NOW WE HAVE TO LOOK OUT FOR HIM ALL DAY AND HE DOESN'T EVEN WANT TO BE HERE.

I . . . I CAN WATCH HIM.
WHAT?

YOU GUYS GO.
I'LL HANG OUT WITH HIM. TEXT ME LATER WHEN YOU WANT TO MEET UP.

ARE YOU SURE?
I'LL BE FINE.

YEAH, THAT'S DEFINITELY HIM!
OH! THE CEMETERY GUY FROM THE INTERNET!
LET'S! GO!

THANKS, JACKIE.
BE GOOD, CALEB.

WHAT ARE YOU READING?
YOU WOULDN'T LIKE IT.
YOU DON'T KNOW THAT.

IT'S CALIFORNIA HISTORY. EARLY 1900S.
MOSTLY STUFF ABOUT KOREAN IMMIGRATION TO SAN FRANCISCO AND LOS ANGELES.

WELL, IF YOU LIKE EARLY 1900S CALIFORNIA HISTORY, I CAN SHOW YOU SOMETHING PRETTY COOL.
REALLY?
FOLLOW ME.

THIS IS HISTORY HALL, BUT MOST PEOPLE JUST CALL IT THE HISTORY CENTER.
COME ON.

ANYTHING ON THE HISTORY OF THE PARK AND KINGDOM ADVENTURE, YOU CAN FIND IN HERE. AND SINCE IT ALL STARTED WITH ANIMATION IN CALIFORNIA, THEY HAVE STUFF THAT DATES BACK TO THE 1930S.
INTERESTING.
THIS IS SOME OF MY FAVORITE STUFF.

"SEE, WAY BACK IN THE THIRTIES, THIS ANIMATOR NAMED PATTY BOONE WAS SICK OF NOT BEING TAKEN SERIOUSLY BECAUSE SHE WAS A WOMAN."

"SO SHE CHANGED HER NAME TO P. J. BOONE. SHE WOULD SEND HER ANIMATION OUT TO DIFFERENT COMPANIES UNDER THAT NAME, AND PEOPLE WATCHED THEM, NOT KNOWING SHE WAS A WOMAN."

"THIS IS THE ONE THAT REALLY GOT PEOPLE'S ATTENTION."
The Escape

"IT WAS ABOUT A PRINCESS NAMED BRIANNA WHO WAS HELD CAPTIVE IN A CASTLE BY THE EVIL DRAGON ELDRIC."

"AT FIRST, SHE'S HELPLESS. SHE WAITS AROUND FOR A PRINCE TO SAVE HER, BUT NOT FOR VERY LONG."

"SHE GETS AN IDEA FROM SEEING THE LARGE DRAGON SCALES THAT ELDRIC HAS AND PUTS A PLAN TOGETHER TO SAVE HERSELF."

"IT WAS GROUNDBREAKING BECAUSE SO MANY CARTOONS AT THE TIME FEATURED DAMSELS IN DISTRESS. AND BRIANNA WAS THE EXACT OPPOSITE."

"THIS WAS ALSO THE INTRODUCTION OF UNICORN HENRY, A MAGICAL CREATURE SHE FOUND AFTER ESCAPING AND RODE AWAY ON TO FREEDOM. AND THAT WAS THE BEGINNING OF THE WHOLE KINGDOM ADVENTURE EMPIRE."

"BOONE KEPT MAKING CARTOONS AND ADDED MORE CHARACTERS. THEY ALL NEEDED A PLACE TO LIVE, SO IT DEVELOPED OVER TIME, AND EVENTUALLY THEY EXPANDED TO MERCHANDISE AND THEN BUILT THIS PLACE, LIKE IN THE SIXTIES, I THINK."

"SOME OF THE OTHER CARTOONS ARE FUN. MY FAVORITES ARE THE ONES ABOUT THE WITCH."

WHY DID PEOPLE CARE THAT THE ARTIST WAS A WOMAN?
WOMEN DIDN'T DO MUCH IN ANIMATION BACK IN THE THIRTIES.
WOMEN WEREN'T REALLY ALLOWED TO DO MUCH OF ANYTHING IN THE THIRTIES OUTSIDE OF HOUSEWORK AND RAISING KIDS.

MY BOOK SAYS A LOT OF WOMEN WORKED ON PLANES AND STUFF DURING SOME WAR.
YEP, AND THEY SENT THEM ALL BACK HOME AFTER THAT WAR. I SAW A BASEBALL MOVIE ABOUT IT ONCE.
HEY, ARE YOU HUNGRY?

THANK YOU.
The Cinnamon Blade

COME ON, LET'S TAKE A WALK.

MOST THEME PARKS ARE SET UP LIKE A PIZZA OR A WAGON WHEEL. KINGDOM ADVENTURE'S ONE OF THOSE. ONCE YOU START AT THE CASTLE AND HEAD NORTH, YOU RUN INTO FAIRY LAND.
EVERYTHING THERE IS OVERSIZED TO MAKE YOU FEEL TINY. THERE'S A COOL TREE HOUSE NEIGHBORHOOD THING IN THERE, TOO. A FUN STORE WHERE YOU CAN GET SOME WINGS AND WANDS.
COOL.

IF YOU HEAD COUNTERCLOCKWISE, YOU HIT THE UNICORN GLEN. IT'S SUPPOSED TO BE THE HOME OF UNICORN HENRY, BUT THE COSTUMED CHARACTER ONLY COMES OUT ONCE A DAY FOR PHOTOS.
IT'S A PRETTY, GRASSY, OPEN AREA WITH HEDGE MAZES AND A PLACE TO EAT, AND A BEAUTIFUL LAKE. THERE'RE HOLOGRAPHIC FANTASY CREATURES, TOO.
HMM.

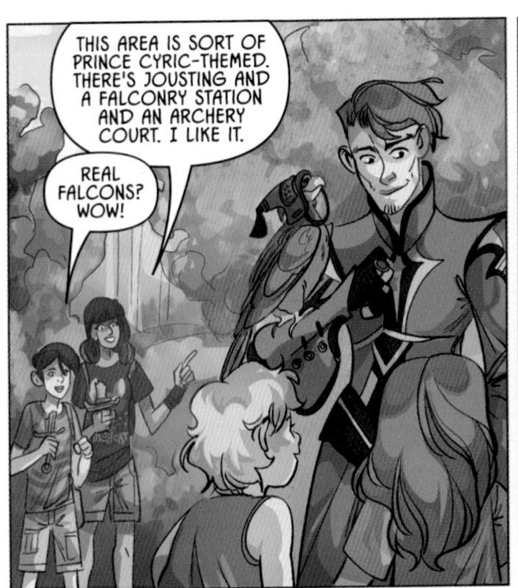
THIS AREA IS SORT OF PRINCE CYRIC-THEMED. THERE'S JOUSTING AND A FALCONRY STATION AND AN ARCHERY COURT. I LIKE IT.
REAL FALCONS? WOW!

THEN YOU CROSS OVER WHERE A BUNCH OF THE STORES ARE, NEAR THE FRONT ENTRANCE.
WITCHCAT

RIGHT BY THE HISTORY CENTER IS THE PARK'S LARGEST ATTRACTION, ELDRIC'S SPINE. REMEMBER THE DRAGON THAT KIDNAPPED BRIANNA?
YEAH.
WELL, THAT'S HIM. I'M NOT A HUGE FAN. I ALWAYS THINK SOMETHING'S GONNA FALL OUT OF MY POCKETS WHEN IT GOES UPSIDE DOWN.

AND I SAVED THE BEST FOR LAST. MY FAVORITE AREA, THE HAUNTED FOREST! IT'S THE HOME OF THE WITCH GITA AND THE WIZARD GOWAN.
GITA'S HOUSE IS A COOL HAUNTED-HOUSE THING. THE WIZARD LIVES IN A BIG CAVE YOU CAN VISIT AND WALK THROUGH, BUT IT'S BASICALLY A GIFT SHOP.
I GOT A CAULDRON THERE WHEN I WAS SIX, AND I STILL HAVE IT.
AWESOME!

THANK YOU.

LET'S SIT. THAT WAS QUITE A WALK.

THANKS FOR THE LIMEADE. AND THE CHURRO.
YOU'RE WELCOME. THEY'RE TWO OF MY FAVORITE THINGS TO GET HERE.
YOU KNOW SO MUCH ABOUT THIS PLACE. SORRY YOU GOT STUCK WITH ME.

HONESTLY, KID, YOU'RE DOING ME A FAVOR. I KIND OF WANTED TO BE ALONE TODAY, SO HANGING OUT WITH YOU IS BETTER THAN BEING WITH THE REST OF THE GROUP.

WHY DID YOU WANT TO COME HERE AND BE . . . ALONE?
THIS PLACE MEANS A LOT TO ME. IT'S A LONG STORY.
REALLY? THIS DOESN'T SEEM LIKE YOUR KIND OF PLACE. EVERYONE HERE IS, LIKE, OVERLY HAPPY AND EXCITED, AND YOU'RE, WELL . . .
PLEASE CONTINUE . . .

WELL, YOU KNOW.

WHAT ABOUT YOU? WHEN WE GOT HERE YOU WERE ALL, "OH, THIS PLACE IS STUPID, THIS IS A WASTE OF TIME, I'M JUST GONNA READ, BLAH BLAH."

I DON'T KNOW. I'M ADOPTED, AND IT'S OBVIOUS. I MEAN, I'M KOREAN. PEOPLE POINT OUT ALL THE TIME THAT I DON'T LOOK LIKE MY FAMILY. I GET SICK OF HEARING IT, SO I JUST STAY QUIET AND READ A LOT.
I'M SHY.

DUDE, I'M SHY, TOO. I BARELY KNOW YOUR BROTHER AND WE'VE HUNG OUT FOR A COUPLE YEARS NOW. I GUESS HE'S MORE NIKKI'S FRIEND.
BUT THERE'S NOTHING WRONG WITH BEING SHY.

YOU DON'T SEEM SHY TO ME. YOU JUST SHOWED ME A BUNCH OF THE PARK. YOU BOUGHT ME LIMEADE AND CHURROS.
THOSE CHURROS **ARE** AMAZING. ONE OF MY FIRST MEMORIES IS SITTING ON THIS SAME BENCH WITH MY DAD, EATING ONE AND WATCHING KIDS TAKE PHOTOS WITH PRINCESS BRIANNA.

HE'D BUY ME ONE EVERY TIME WE CAME HERE. I'D SPLIT IT WITH MY MOM. SIT HERE AND JUST STARE AT THE PRINCESS AND WATCH HOW HAPPY SHE MADE EVERYONE.
BUT WHY DON'T YOU COME HERE WITH YOUR PARENTS NOW?

THEY DON'T LIVE HERE ANYMORE.

WHO ARE YOU TEXTING?
NIKKI. I'M ASKING WHERE SHE IS, BUT JUDGING BY THE HOUR, I KNOW SHE'S ALREADY IN THERE TRYING TO GET A PHOTO OP.
ARE THOSE PADDLE BOATS?
YEAH, THEY'RE PRETTY CHILL.
AND THIS IS THE THRONE ROOM WE'RE GOING INTO?
YEAH, IT'S WHERE THE KING, QUEEN, AND PRINCESS BRIANNA POSE FOR PICTURES.
NIKKI ALWAYS WANTS TO GET HER PHOTO WITH BRIANNA. HER INTENSITY ABOUT IT IS NEXT LEVEL.
JUST WATCH.

THERE YOU ARE.
I TEXTED YOU THAT WE WERE ON OUR WAY.
DID CALEB BEHAVE?

THIS ALWAYS TAKES FOREVER.

NO! SHE'S LEAVING! THIS SUCKS!
SHE DOESN'T COME OUT FOR PHOTOS FOR AT LEAST ANOTHER TWO HOURS!

JACKIE! LOOK!
OH NO. HER DRESS. THAT'S NOT GOOD.
THAT'S GOTTA BE, LIKE, A FIREABLE OFFENSE. TO BE EXPOSED LIKE THAT AND NOT COSTUME-READY FOR YOUR WHOLE PHOTO-TAKING SHIFT.
COME ON!
WHAT? WHERE?

LOOK, THE CASTLE GUARD SECURITY PERSON IS LEAVING HIS POST, AND BRIANNA IS LIKELY GOING ON A BREAK. THAT MEANS SHE'S HEADING INTO THE SECRET TUNNELS UNDERNEATH THE PARK.
DO YOU SEE WHERE I'M GOING HERE?

I *DO* WANNA SEE THAT.

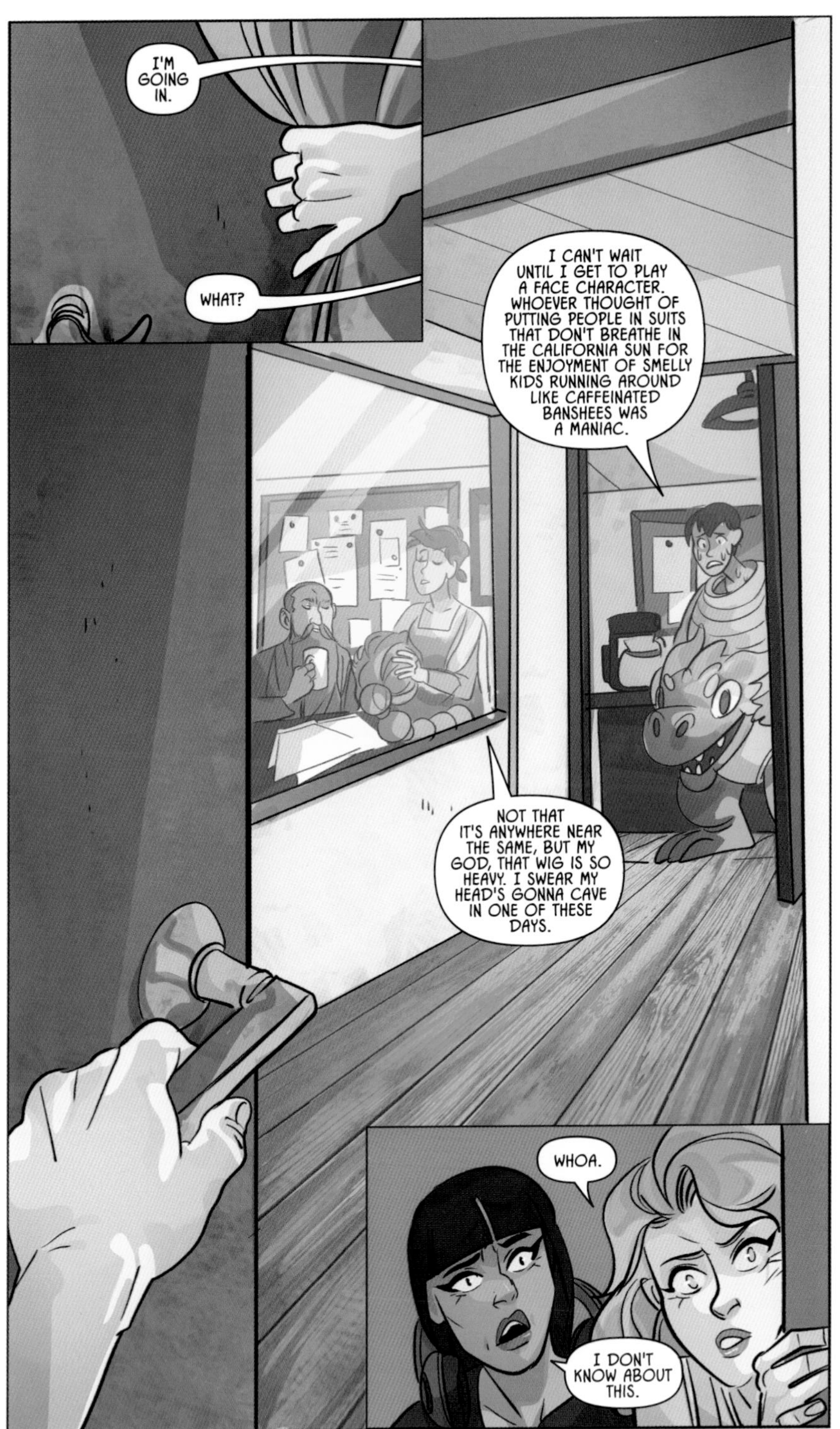
I'M GOING IN.
WHAT?
I CAN'T WAIT UNTIL I GET TO PLAY A FACE CHARACTER. WHOEVER THOUGHT OF PUTTING PEOPLE IN SUITS THAT DON'T BREATHE IN THE CALIFORNIA SUN FOR THE ENJOYMENT OF SMELLY KIDS RUNNING AROUND LIKE CAFFEINATED BANSHEES WAS A MANIAC.
NOT THAT IT'S ANYWHERE NEAR THE SAME, BUT MY GOD, THAT WIG IS SO HEAVY. I SWEAR MY HEAD'S GONNA CAVE IN ONE OF THESE DAYS.
WHOA.
I DON'T KNOW ABOUT THIS.

I FEEL LIKE I'M SWEATING OUT TEN POUNDS EVERY SHIFT.
AT LEAST YOU'VE GOT A FAN INSIDE OF THAT BIG FOAM HEAD.

THIS.
IS.
AMAZING.

NIKK, ANYONE COULD COME AROUND THE CORNER AT ANY TIME. WE SHOULD GO.

DID YOU HEAR ABOUT TOKYO?
ABOUT THE NEW PARK THERE? YEAH, OF COURSE.

WHAT? WHAT DID SHE JUST SAY? A NEW PARK?
QUIET! I'M TRYING TO LISTEN!

NO, I MEAN THE GUY WHO FELL. THEY WERE TESTING OUT A NEW ATTRACTION SPECIFICALLY FOR THAT PARK AND SOME-ONE DIED.
THEY'RE KEEPING IT QUIET, OF COURSE.

THAT'S WILD. ABOUT FIVE YEARS AGO HERE, SOMEONE HAD A HEART ATTACK AND DIED. THEY WERE, LIKE, CRAZY OLD.

AND THE COMPANY GAVE THE WHOLE GROUP THAT WAS WITH THE DECEASED LIFETIME PASSES TO THE PARK. APPARENTLY, IT'S SOMETHING THEY DO TO AVOID A LOT OF LEGAL TROUBLE.
IS THAT TRUE?
I MEAN, IT'S JUST WHAT I'VE HEARD. JESUS, I'D KILL FOR A CIGARETTE RIGHT NOW.

YEAH, MY BREAK'S OVER. I'M TAKING OVER FOR PHIL.
OH NO.
LET'S GO WHILE WE CAN.

COME ON!

THAT WAS CLOSE.
DING DING!

WHERE DID YOU TWO GO?
WE SAW THE UNDERGROUND TUNNELS! WHERE THE COSTUME CHARACTERS TAKE BREAKS!

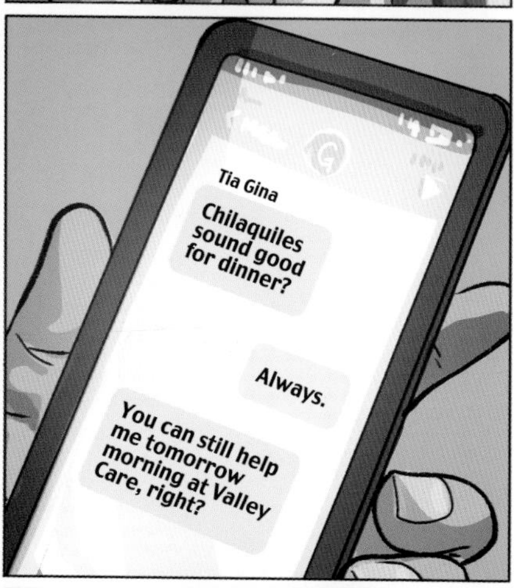
Tia Gina
Chilaquiles sound good for dinner?
Always.
You can still help me tomorrow morning at Valley Care, right?

WHO'S THAT?
HUH? OH, UH . . . JUST MY AUNT.

COME OVER TO MY PLACE TONIGHT, GUYS.
I HAVE A CRAZY IDEA.

CAN HE HEAR US?
THEY'RE NOISE-CANCELLING HEADPHONES, AND HE'S PLAYING A GAME. HE CAN'T HEAR ANYTHING.
WHAT'S WITH ALL THESE MEETINGS? CAN'T WE JUST CHILL LIKE–

DAMNIT! ANOTHER NASTY ARTICLE JUST CAME OUT. PEOPLE NEED TO GET OVER IT!

SO, NIKKI AND I DISCOVERED SOMETHING ABOUT THE PARK TODAY THAT I THINK YOU'LL WANNA HEAR.

WE OVERHEARD SOME EMPLOYEES TALKING ON A BREAK. APPARENTLY, IF A MEMBER OF YOUR PARTY DIES WHILE AT KINGDOM ADVENTURE, TO AVOID A LOT OF LEGAL TROUBLE, THE COMPANY WILL GIVE THE REST OF THE PARTY LIFETIME PASSES.

WHAT? THAT CAN'T BE REAL.

IT HAS TO BE.

I'VE BEEN LOOKING ONLINE. I CAN'T FIND ANYTHING PROVING IT, BUT WE HEARD BRIANNA TALKING ABOUT IT.
I ***DID*** FIND AN ARTICLE SAYING THAT TEN YEARS AGO, A BUNCH OF PARKGOERS CONTRACTED MEASLES WHILE THEY WERE THERE, AND SOMEONE LET IT SLIP THAT THEY WERE ALL GIVEN PASSES.

WHAT'S THAT GOT TO DO WITH ***US?***

I WON'T BE ABLE TO GO TO THE PARK MUCH LONGER. THE SEASONAL AND YEARLY PASSES ARE TOO EXPENSIVE, AND MY AUNT CAN'T AFFORD IT.

THAT DIDN'T ANSWER MY QUESTION.
WELL, YOU NEED TO REBRAND YOUR IMAGE, RIGHT?

AND NIKKI, YOU WANT FULL ACCESS TO THE PARK WHENEVER YOU FEEL LIKE IT FOR RESEARCH, OBSERVING BRIANNA AND THE COSTUMED CHARACTERS.
BRIANNA, YES.

AND IF YOU'RE GONNA TRY OUT FOR CYRIC WITH NIKKI ONE DAY, IT MIGHT BE HELPFUL . . .
YEAH, I GUESS SO.

WELL, MY AUNT IS THE HEAD NURSE AT VALLEY CARE LIVING. I HELP HER OUT WITH CLEANING AND STUFF WHEN SHE'S SHORT-STAFFED.
SO, WHAT IF WE START, LIKE, A FAKE VOLUNTEER PROGRAM TO TAKE THE ELDERLY TO THE PARK ONCE OR TWICE A WEEK. WHILE WE'RE THERE . . . ONE OF THEM MIGHT . . .

DIE?

WELL, YEAH. IT'S NOT LIKE ANY OF THEM ARE DOING ANYTHING IMPORTANT AT VALLEY CARE, ANYWAY. THEY PRETTY MUCH JUST SIT THERE ALL DAY.

I DON'T KNOW. I MEAN, WE HAVE PASSES, BUT HOW ARE WE SUPPOSED TO PAY FOR SOMEONE ELSE TO GO ALL THE TIME?

WELL, IF WE FORM THE PROGRAM AND APPEAL TO THE SENIOR-CITIZEN PLACE, THEY MIGHT PAY FOR IT, YOU NEVER KNOW. WE'RE DOING THEM A FAVOR, ENTERTAINING THEIR BORED, WRINKLY OLD RESIDENTS.
THIS IS GOOD. THEY'D BE, YOU KNOW . . . HAVING FUN. IT'S NOT LIKE WE'RE TALKING ABOUT MURDER HERE.

OH! I COULD FILM MYSELF AT THE PARK WITH THESE FOGIES. MAKE EVERYONE THINK I'M DOING SOMETHING GOOD.
I MIGHT KEEP THE SPONSORSHIP FOR MY CHANNEL.
EXACTLY.

I COULD EVEN MAKE A TEARFUL GOODBYE VIDEO TO WHOEVER IT IS THAT DIES . . .

. . . AND THEN, LIKE, MAYBE EVEN REVEAL THAT CRAZY RULE.

OH, I'D GET SO MANY NEW FOLLOWERS. NOBODY WOULD DARE CANCEL ME.

I'M IN. I'M *SO* IN.

SO WE'RE DOING THIS? WE'RE ALL IN? NIKKI?

I'M DEFINITELY IN.

I GUESS TO GET STARTED, YOU'LL NEED TO TALK TO YOUR AUNT OR WHOEVER IS IN CHARGE AT VALLEY CARE, RIGHT? MAYBE EVEN COME UP WITH A PHONY NAME FOR THE PROGRAM.

SHE'S WORKING LATE TONIGHT, BUT I'M SUPPOSED TO HELP HER THERE TOMORROW, SO I CAN ASK HER THEN.

IT'LL GIVE ME A BIT MORE TIME TO FLESH THINGS OUT. AND THEN WE CAN GO FROM THERE.

ARE YOU GUYS DONE YET?

YEAH, WE'RE DONE.

THANKS FOR LETTING ME BORROW THOSE, JACKIE. THEY'RE COOL.
SURE.

YOU DIDN'T TELL US YOU HAVE A NEW BOYFRIEND. HOW LONG HAVE YOU TWO BEEN TOGETHER?

SHUT UP, BERKE.

LET'S GO, CALEB.

I'LL GET IN TOUCH WITH YOU GUYS TOMORROW.
SEE YA LATER!

THIS IS GONNA BE SO GREAT!
DENY ME AND BE DOOMED

TÍA GINA, YOU GOT A SECOND?
CLARO, AMOR. WHAT'S UP?
REMEMBER HOW YOU WERE SAYING THAT YOU WANT ME TO DO SOMETHING WITH MY SUMMER? LIKE, OUT IN THE SUN?
I DO.
WELL, I THOUGHT OF SOMETHING I WANNA DO, BUT I HAVE TO ASK YOU ABOUT IT.
WHAT IS IT?

I, WELL, MY FRIENDS AND I, WE WERE HOPING TO TAKE SOME OF THE RESIDENTS HERE TO THE PARK WITH US THIS SUMMER. TO HELP THEM GET SOME FRESH AIR AND DO SOMETHING FUN.
I KNOW IT SOUNDS A LITTLE CRAZY, BUT I'LL BE USING MY PASS A LOT BEFORE IT EXPIRES ANYWAY AND FIGURED, YOU KNOW, THEY DON'T GET OUT A LOT.

OH JACKIE, I DON'T KNOW.
I DON'T THINK MANY OF THE RESIDENTS CAN HANDLE ROLLER COASTERS AND STUFF.

THEY WOULDN'T HAVE TO GO ON ANY OF THE CRAZY OR INTENSE RIDES OR ANYTHING. IT COULD JUST BE, YOU KNOW, TO WALK AROUND, ENJOY THE OUTSIDE.
WELL, I GUESS THAT WOULD BE OKAY.
WE DO HAVE A SMALL ACTIVITIES BUDGET THAT NEVER GETS USED. OUR LAST ACTIVITIES COORDINATOR QUIT A FEW MONTHS AGO, SO THE RESIDENTS HAVEN'T DONE MUCH LATELY. MAYBE WE COULD GET A SUMMER PASS IN VALLEY CARE'S NAME.

REALLY? THAT'S GREAT.

WELL THEN, YOU JUST HAVE TO CLEAR IT WITH THE FACILITIES COORDINATOR, MR. GRABLE. HE SHOULD BE IN HIS OFFICE RIGHT NOW IF YOU WANT TO TRY AND CATCH HIM.
OH. OKAY. THANKS, TÍA.
MEXICANA

MEXICANA

ALL RIGHT, BEST TWO OUT OF THREE.

KNOCK KNOCK KNOCK
COME IN.

A FEW MINUTES LATER . . . .
IT'S AN AWFULLY NICE THING YOU AND YOUR FRIENDS WANT TO DO, THIS . . .
S.T.O.P.: SENIOR TIME OUTREACH PROGRAM.
RIGHT. YES, BUT I'M NOT SURE OUR RESIDENTS SHOULD BE RIDING ROLLER COASTERS AND THRILL RIDES.
MY AUNT SAID THE SAME THING. THEY WOULDN'T BE DOING THAT. JUST GOING OUT IN THE AIR, ENJOYING THE SCENERY, MAYBE GOING ON SOME OF THE SIMPLE KID RIDES.
IF THEY WANT TO, THAT IS.
WELL, THAT SOUNDS ALL RIGHT, I SUPPOSE.

SO WHAT NEEDS TO HAPPEN IN ORDER FOR MY FRIENDS AND I TO TAKE RESIDENTS? DO WE NEED, LIKE, PAPERWORK OR PERMISSION SLIPS?
VERY LITTLE, ACTUALLY. THE RESIDENTS, WELL, THEY'RE ALL ADULTS. I'D SAY, SEE IF THERE'S ANY VOLUNTEERS AND ASK AROUND TO SEE IF ANYONE WANTS TO GO. THEN START A SCHEDULE.
THAT'S IT?
ALMOST.
WON'T YOU EXCUSE ME, HELEN? I'LL BE RIGHT BACK.
MY AUNT MENTIONED THE EVENTS BUDGET . . .
I THINK WE COULD DIP INTO IT IF YOU'D BE WILLING TO DO OTHER EVENTS AS WELL.

WHAT DO YOU MEAN?
SIMPLE THINGS. MOVIE NIGHT, BRIDGE TOURNAMENT.
THINGS TO HELP THE RESIDENTS OCCUPY THEIR TIME.

OH, I DON'T KNOW . . . I MEAN, I GUESS.

WE'RE IN NEED OF SOMEONE TO BE AN ACTIVITIES COORDINATOR.
YOU'D HAVE THAT BUDGET, PLUS ACCESS TO THE FACILITIES VAN FOR TRANSPORTING THE RESIDENTS.
AND THIS WOULD PAY FOR THE TICKET PRICE OF WHOEVER YOU TAKE TO THE PARK. SENIOR TICKETS ARE CHEAPER ANYWAY, SO IT SHOULDN'T MAKE TOO BIG OF A DENT IN THE BUDGET.

YOU WANT ME TO BE THE ACTIVITIES COORDINATOR?

YOU'RE SHOWING INITIATIVE WITH THIS PLAN. I DON'T SEE WHY NOT.

WELL, SURE. I MEAN, IF YOU THINK I CAN DO IT.
OF COURSE YOU CAN. WE CAN TALK DETAILS AND EVENTS IN A FEW DAYS.
FOR NOW, HAVE FUN AT KINGDOM ADVENTURE. AND BE SAFE. THE RESIDENTS HERE CAN BE A HANDFUL SOMETIMES!

AHEM.

EXCUSE ME? YOU'RE NURSE GINA'S DAUGHTER?

NIECE. MY NAME'S JACKIE.
MY APOLOGIES. I COULDN'T HELP BUT OVERHEAR THAT LAST BIT OF YOUR CONVERSATION WITH MR. GRABLE.
OH, YOU DID?

YOU'RE STARTING A PROGRAM TO TAKE RESIDENTS TO THE PARK? THE ONE HERE IN TOWN?
YEAH. WITH MY FRIENDS.

THAT'S . . . THAT'S THE IDEA, ANYWAY.
INTERESTING.

I'M COMING WITH YOU.

OH . . . YOU WANT TO GO?
YES. I THINK YOU'D FIND ME TO BE PERFECTLY LOVELY COMPANY.
OUR FIRST TRIP IS TOMORROW. ARE YOU FREE TO GO THEN?
I'LL CHECK MY SCHEDULE AND SEE IF I CAN FIT IT IN. MY DAYS CAN BECOME PRETTY OVERBOOKED IF I'M NOT CAREFUL.
MEXICANA
THAT WAS A JOKE, DARLING.

OH . . . HA. UM, OKAY, I'LL BE HERE TOMORROW AT 10:30. IS THAT TOO EARLY?
I WAKE UP AT SIX.
UM, BRING SUNGLASSES IF YOU HAVE ANY.
I DO.
I'LL BRING SUNBLOCK.
I'LL BRING A PARASOL.

A WHAT?

I'LL SEE YOU AT 10:30, YOUNG LADY.

"SORRY ABOUT THAT, HELEN. LET'S CONTINUE."
"WHAT WAS THAT ALL ABOUT?"

NOTHING . . . JUST SOMETHING I HAD TO DO.

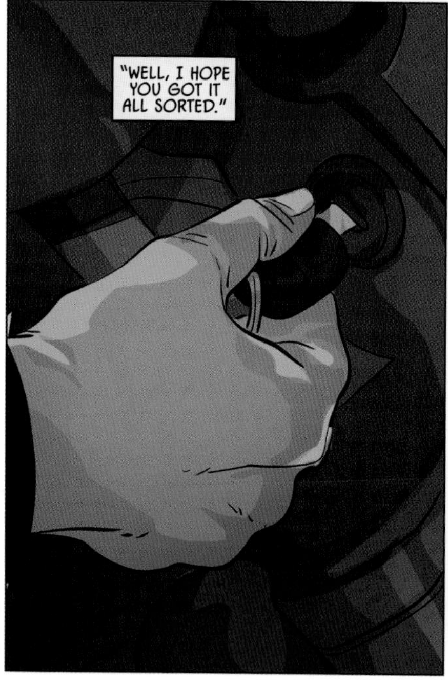
"WELL, I HOPE YOU GOT IT ALL SORTED."

"I THINK IT WILL BE SOON."

TAKE GOOD CARE OF HER, JACKIE.
I'LL BE FINE, DEAR.
BRING HER BACK IN ONE PIECE, NOW.

HAVE HER BACK BY SUNDOWN, JACKIE. AND MAKE SURE YOU BOTH EAT SOMETHING.
NOT JUNK FOOD EITHER.
UH, IT'S A THEME PARK.

TAKE THIS, TOO. THAT WAY, SHE WON'T HAVE TO WALK TOO FAR.
OH, OKAY.

HAVE FUN. BE SAFE.
WE WILL.

GOODBYE, BEAUTIFUL.

ALLEN, FOR THE LOVE OF GOD.

READY?

EMPHATICALLY.

LET'S GO.

WHAT ABOUT YOUR FRIENDS?

HUH?
YOUR FRIENDS.
YOU ARE ALL A PART OF THIS PROGRAM? TO TAKE US TO THE PARK?
THIS . . . S.T.O.P.?

OH, YEAH. WE ARE.

ARE WE PICKING THEM UP OR MEETING THEM AT THE PARK, DEAR?

OH, THEY'RE MEETING US THERE.
LOOKS LIKE.
HMMM. SO YOU WERE TASKED WITH CHAUFFEURING?

WELCOME
IT'S NOT AS FULL AS I EXPECTED IT TO BE.
THURSDAY IS THE LEAST-BUSIEST DAY AT THE PARK. IT'LL FILL UP WITHIN THE NEXT HOUR OR SO.
I, UH . . . I'LL COME AROUND AND GET THE DOOR FOR YOU, I GUESS.
HOW REFRESHING. A YOUNG PERSON WITH MANNERS.

THANK YOU, DARLING.

TO THE TICKET BOOTH?
I ALREADY GOT YOUR TICKET ONLINE. IT'S ON MY PHONE. WE JUST SHOW THEM TO SECURITY.
TICKET ON YOUR PHONE? IF YOU SAY SO.

I'M SORRY THE ENTRANCE ISN'T CLOSER.
IT'S NOT A PROBLEM. PLEASE DON'T WORRY.

WELCOME, ONE AND ALL, TO KINGDOM ADVENTURE! PLEASE HAVE YOUR BAGS AND PURSES OPEN AS YOU COME THROUGH!

SNIFF

MRS. ADLER? ARE YOU OKAY?

I'M PERFECTLY FINE. IT'S JUST ALLERGIES.

READY?

LET'S GO.

THERE THEY ARE.

OH, DEAR ME. CURSE THIS THING.

LET ME CLOSE THIS UP. I APOLOGIZE.
IT'S FINE, MA'AM. WE JUST NEED TO SEE INSIDE YOUR PURSE.

OH, OF COURSE, OF COURSE.
AM I TO PREPARE MYSELF TO BE GROPED AS WELL?

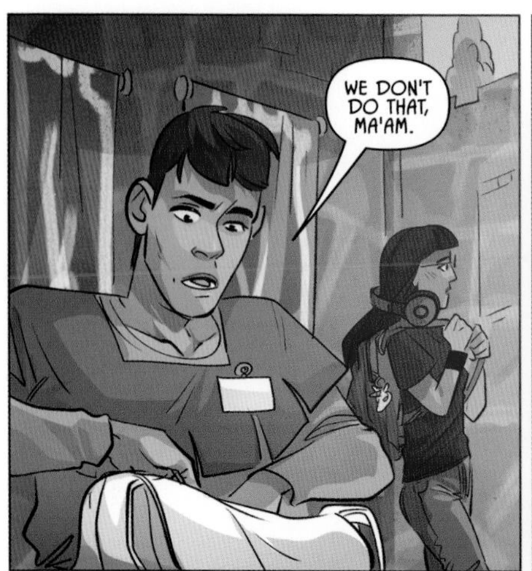
WE DON'T DO THAT, MA'AM.

GOOD TO KNOW.

FINALLY!
I MEAN, I KNEW OLD PEOPLE WERE SLOW, BUT COME ON. WE'VE BEEN WAITING HERE FOREVER.

HI, EVERYONE, I'M HERE AT KINGDOM ADVENTURE ON THIS BEAUTIFUL, SUNNY CALIFORNIA DAY WITH MY NEW FRIEND. THIS IS SOMETHING I'VE BEEN WANTING TO DO FOR A **REALLY** LONG TIME, AND I–

GREAT, YOU COULDN'T SMILE, LADY? I'M GONNA HAVE TO RESHOOT THAT NOW.
SIR! SELFIE STICKS ARE NOT ALLOWED! I'M GOING TO NEED TO CONFISCATE THAT!

OKAY, WELL, HERE'S WHAT I'M THINKING. IF WE HIT UP ELDRIC'S SPINE AND THE WITCH'S HOUSE RIDE FIRST, THEN WE'LL GET THROUGH THEM BEFORE THE PARK FILLS UP.

HOW DID YOU GET THIS IN HERE?

IT WAS JUST IN MY POCKET, MAN. YOU BETTER GIVE IT BACK WHEN I LEAVE.

THOSE TWO RIDES USUALLY HAVE THE LONGEST WAIT TIMES, SO IT'S BEST TO GET THEM OUT OF THE WAY.

THEN WE CAN GO THROUGH THE WIZARD'S CAVE, AND AFTER THAT, HEAD OVER TO THE MAGIC PAVILION FOR THEIR SHOW IN FAIRY LAND.

AND WE CAN SEE THE HOLOGRAPHIC CREATURES IN THE UNICORN GLEN AND RUN OVER TO THE FALCONRY STATION IN THE KING'S CORNER. THEN WE CAN SEE THE JOUSTING TOURNAMENT AROUND LUNCHTIME.
I CAN'T BELIEVE HE TOOK MY SELFIE STICK. NOW I ACTUALLY GOTTA HOLD MY PHONE IN MY HAND!

I FIND IT AMUSING AND FLATTERING THAT YOU THINK I'M ABLE AND WILLING TO DO ALL OF THAT, MY DEAR.
I WILL GO ON THE FERRIS WHEEL BEFORE LUNCH, AND THAT'S JUST ABOUT ALL.

WHATEVER. AT LEAST I CAN GET SOME GOOD SHOTS OF THE PARK FROM UP THERE.
of the Gryphon
YOU AREN'T AFRAID OF HEIGHTS OR ANYTHING, ARE YOU, MRS. ADLER?

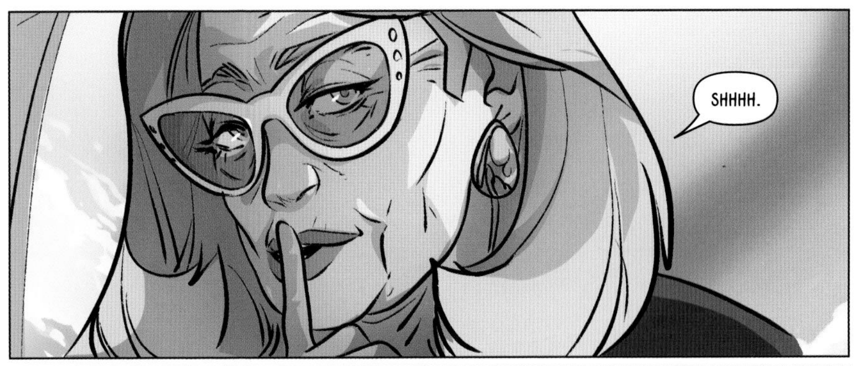

JUST TAKE IN THE VIEW.

OKAY, THAT WAS THRILLING, BUT I'M GOING ON THE ROLLER COASTER NOW.
MEXICANA

COME ON, ELDRIC'S SPINE ISN'T A LONG WALK, BUT . . .
THERE'S A TRAIN. WE'LL TAKE THAT.

UGH, LADY, YOU'RE KILLING ME!
FINE.

YOU CAN GET SHOTS OF THE WHOLE PARK AT EYE LEVEL FOR YOUR LITTLE MOVIE IF WE TAKE IT NORTH, YOUNG MAN.

WHATEVER.

YOUNG LADY, THERE'S SOMETHING I DON'T QUITE UNDERSTAND.
WHAT'S THAT?
THIS KINDNESS, THIS WILLINGNESS TO BRING VALLEY CARE RESIDENTS TO THE PARK, IT'S VERY THOUGHTFUL.

OH, THANKS.

YES, WELL, PARDON MY IMPERTINENCE, BUT IT DOESN'T SEEM LIKE SOMETHING YOU OR YOUR FRIENDS ARE ESPECIALLY HAPPY TO DO.

WELL, SORRY IF I COME OFF RUDE AND UNHAPPY.

THAT'S USUALLY A BY-PRODUCT OF BEING RUDE AND UNHAPPY.

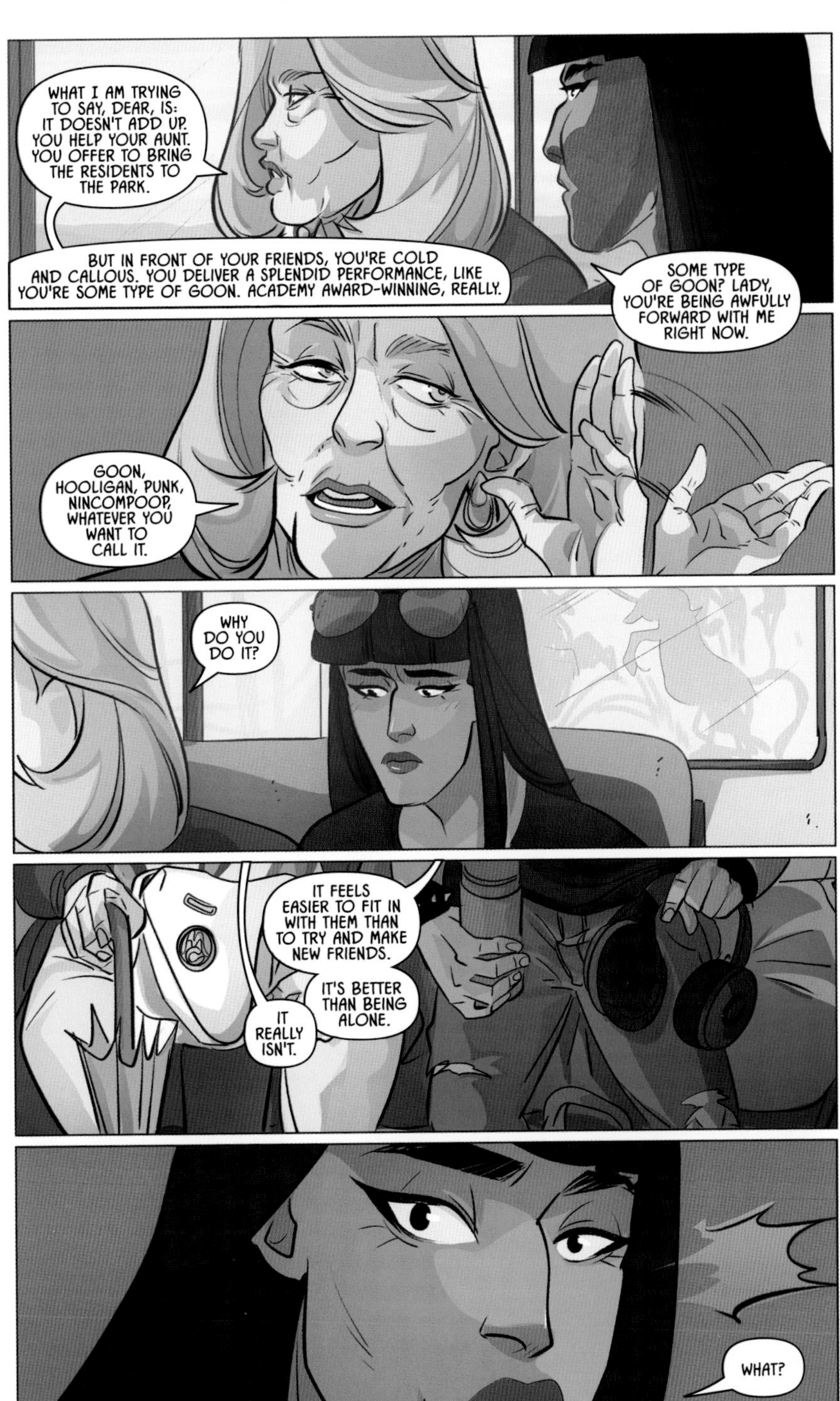
WHAT I AM TRYING TO SAY, DEAR, IS: IT DOESN'T ADD UP. YOU HELP YOUR AUNT. YOU OFFER TO BRING THE RESIDENTS TO THE PARK.
BUT IN FRONT OF YOUR FRIENDS, YOU'RE COLD AND CALLOUS. YOU DELIVER A SPLENDID PERFORMANCE, LIKE YOU'RE SOME TYPE OF GOON. ACADEMY AWARD-WINNING, REALLY.
SOME TYPE OF GOON? LADY, YOU'RE BEING AWFULLY FORWARD WITH ME RIGHT NOW.
GOON, HOOLIGAN, PUNK, NINCOMPOOP, WHATEVER YOU WANT TO CALL IT.
WHY DO YOU DO IT?
IT FEELS EASIER TO FIT IN WITH THEM THAN TO TRY AND MAKE NEW FRIENDS.
IT'S BETTER THAN BEING ALONE.
IT REALLY ISN'T.
WHAT?

LISTEN, JACKIE. ONE DAY YOU WAKE UP, YOU LOOK IN THE MIRROR, AND YOU FIND THAT YOU'VE GROWN OLD. YOU BEGIN TO THINK ABOUT WHAT YOU HAVE SPENT YOUR TIME DOING.
YOU THINK ABOUT WHO YOU SPENT THAT TIME WITH, AND YOU REALIZE THAT THE MOST VALUABLE THING IN THIS WORLD, IN THIS LIFE . . . IS *TIME*.
IT'S SOMETHING YOU WILL NEVER GET BACK.
SO YOU REALIZE THAT WHAT AND WHO YOU SPENT THAT TIME ON AND WITH WAS IMPORTANT. TOO IMPORTANT TO THROW AWAY ON PEOPLE WHO DON'T CARE ABOUT YOU.
PEOPLE WHO WILL TAKE AND GIVE NOTHING IN RETURN. THAT'S NOT FRIENDSHIP.
AND YOU DESERVE BETTER.
BUT I DON'T SAY A WORD. IT'S NONE OF MY . . . NEVERMIND.

YEAH? AND JUST WHAT MAKES YOU SO SURE I'M NOT SOME HORRIBLE PERSON?
A . . . GOON, LIKE YOU SAID?
I MEAN, YOU DON'T REALLY KNOW WHAT KIND OF PERSON I AM.

I BELIEVE I DO.

LOOKS LIKE OUR STOP IS COMING UP.

DO YOU ALWAYS WEAR THOSE THINGS, DEAR?

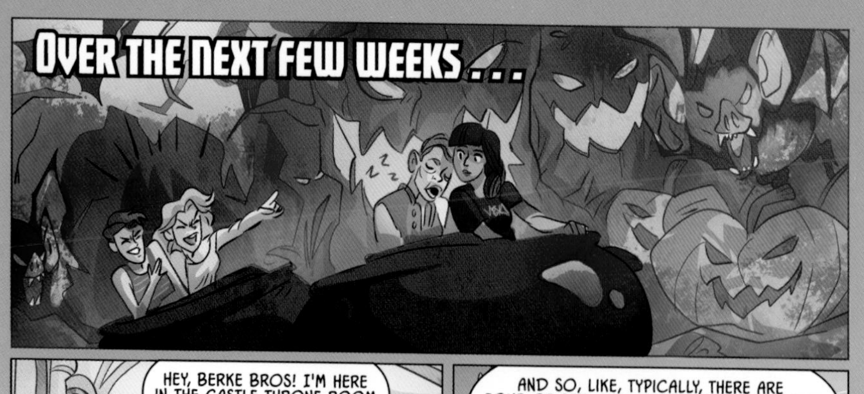
OVER THE NEXT FEW WEEKS . . .
Z Z Z

HEY, BERKE BROS! I'M HERE IN THE CASTLE THRONE ROOM WITH S.T.O.P. AND MY NEW FRIEND GEORGE!
WHY ARE YOU TOUCHING ME?

AND SO, LIKE, TYPICALLY, THERE ARE FOUR OR FIVE CAST MEMBERS WHO PERFORM PRINCESS BRIANNA BECAUSE, YOU KNOW, SHIFTS AND BREAKS AND STUFF, AND WHEN ONE OF THEM GOES ON BREAK, THE ROTATION STARTS. BUT, LIKE, USUALLY . . .

THEY SHOULD LET US TO THE FRONT OF MOST OF THE RIDE LINES SINCE SHE'S IN A WHEELCHAIR.
SHOULD HAVE THOUGHT OF THIS SOONER!

YOU'RE CRAZY IF YOU THINK I'M CLIMBING UP THAT.
DO YOU NOT SEE MY CANE, SON?
UGH! YOU'RE GONNA RUIN THE SHOT I NEED TO GET WITH YOU!
HEY, IS THIS YOUR GRANDMA? YOU GUYS WANNA JOIN US?
OH WOW. PEOPLE ARE SAYING THAT YESTERDAY, ELDRIC'S SPINE ALMOST STARTED WITHOUT EVERYONE BEING FULLY STRAPPED IN. IT'S TRENDING!
THAT WOULD HAVE BEEN SO AWESOME.

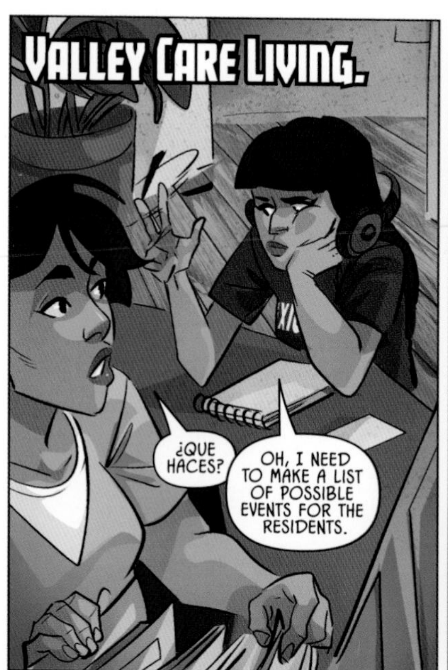
VALLEY CARE LIVING.
¿QUE HACES?
OH, I NEED TO MAKE A LIST OF POSSIBLE EVENTS FOR THE RESIDENTS.

YEAH? LIKE WHAT?

OH, LIKE A GAME NIGHT, BUT THAT SEEMS PRETTY STANDARD. I'M TRYING TO THINK OF OTHER FUN THINGS.
MAYBE A MOVIE NIGHT WITH, LIKE, A POPCORN MACHINE, DRAG QUEEN BINGO. I DON'T KNOW.

I READ SPENDING TIME WITH EMOTIONAL SUPPORT DOGS CAN LIFT PEOPLE'S MOODS.

IT'S VERY NICE OF YOU. EVERYONE HERE WILL REALLY APPRECIATE IT.
THANKS, IT'S A LOT OF PLANNING AND PHONE CALLS.
YOU COULD PLAY YOUR GUITAR FOR THEM.

YEAH, I GUESS I COULD.

ANYWAY, I'M ALSO WAITING FOR ALLEN. IT'S HIS TURN TO GO TO THE PARK AGAIN.
I'LL GO FIND HIM FOR YOU.

DING DING!

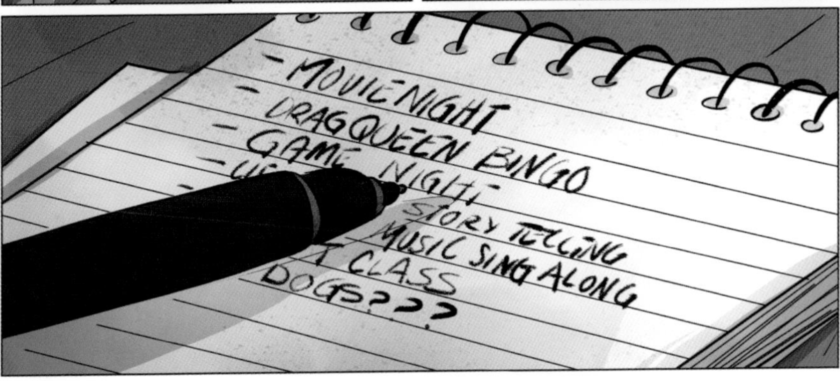
- MOVIE NIGHT
- DRAG QUEEN BINGO
- GAME NIGHT
STORY TELLING
MUSIC SING ALONG
CLASS
DOGS???

LOOK WHO I FOUND.

NOBODY SAID YOU FELL ASLEEP.
I WASN'T SLEEPING. I WAS JUST RESTING MY EYES.

HI, ALLEN. YOU READY?
MEXIC

ABSOLUTELY.
HOLD ON A MINUTE.

I'M JOINING YOU TODAY.

OH, HEY, PHYLLIS. UM, TODAY IS ALLEN'S TURN.
MEXICANI

I REALIZE THAT. I'LL PAY FOR MY OWN TICKET. I JUST NEED A RIDE.
CAN'T STAND TO BE AWAY FROM ME FOR EVEN JUST A SHORT AMOUNT OF TIME?
CONTAIN YOURSELF.

TÍA, IS THAT OKAY?
I DON'T KNOW. IF THERE'S FOUR OF YOU KIDS, I SUPPOSE THAT'S ENOUGH TO WATCH OUT FOR THE TWO OF THEM.

YOUNG LADY, I AM AN ADULT. I HAVE NO NEED FOR A SITTER.

I'M SORRY.

I WASN'T TALKING TO YOU.

IS THERE ANYTHING ABOUT MY MENTAL OR PHYSICAL CONDITION THAT TELLS YOU I SHOULD NOT BE OUTSIDE TODAY?

NO, MRS. ADLER.

THEN THERE ISN'T REALLY A PROBLEM, IS THERE?

I SUPPOSE NOT.

THEN I'LL BE BACK LATER.
WELL, GO QUICKLY, BEFORE THE OTHER RESIDENTS ALL ASK TO JOIN YOU.

SPLENDID.
HOP TO, JACKIE.

WHY DOES IT ALWAYS TAKE YOU FOREVER TO GET THROUGH SECURITY?
GOD, NO KIDDING.

YOUNG MAN, YOU ASK ME THIS EVERY TIME. DO ME A SMALL FAVOR AND KEEP THIS RESPONSE FIRMLY LODGED IN YOUR MIND SO WE DON'T HAVE TO ENDURE THIS CONVERSATION AGAIN . . .
I GO AT MY OWN PACE. NOT YOURS.
SHOW A LITTLE RESPECT FOR YOUR ELDERS, SON.

UH-HUH, SURE.

HE MADE YOU SIT IN A WHEELCHAIR YET?
HE DOESN'T MAKE ME DO *ANYTHING.*

THEY'RE JUST GOING TO SLOW US DOWN. I MEAN, NOW THERE'S TWO OF THEM.
IF ANYTHING HAPPENS TO ONE OF THEM, TECHNICALLY WE ARE STILL A PART OF THEIR GROUP. IT'S NOT LIKE WE HAVE TO BE **WITH** THEM WITH THEM.
BEAST

THAT'S TRUE. BUT WHAT ABOUT DANIEL?
YOU DON'T ALWAYS HAVE TO HAVE HIM FOLLOW YOU AROUND.
BEAST

UH. NIKKI AND I ARE GONNA GO RIDE THE HAUNTED FOREST RIDE. COUSIN BONDING! WE'LL CATCH YOU GUYS LATER.
BEAST

HAVE FUN!

WAIT-
SO RUDE.
DID YOU REALLY WANT TO SPEND ALL DAY WITH THEM?

I GUESS NOT.
GOOD RIDDANCE. EVERYONE, FOLLOW ME.
EXICAN

WHERE?

THE BEST SPOT IN THE PARK.
THE MOST BEAUTIFUL PLACE IN KINGDOM ADVENTURE.

Unicorn Glen.
LET'S FIND A PLACE TO SIT FOR A WHILE.
WHAT ARE YOU ALWAYS LISTENING TO ON THOSE THINGS?
OH, UH, JUST MUSIC.
YES, DEAR. CLEARLY. WHAT KIND OF MUSIC?
YOU WOULDN'T LIKE IT. IT'S HEAVY METAL.

MMM. I SEE. AND THAT'S YOUR FAVORITE KIND OF MUSIC?
IT'S PRETTY MUCH ALL I LISTEN TO NOW.
AND WHY IS THAT?
MEXICANA

IT'S LOUD.

ALL MUSIC CAN BE LOUD.
IT JUST . . . I DON'T KNOW.
IT KIND OF HELPS ME JUST SHUT IT ALL OUT.

"IT ALL? WHAT DO YOU MEAN?"

THREE YEARS AGO, MY PARENTS GOT DEPORTED. I CAME HOME FROM SCHOOL ONE DAY AND THEY WERE GONE.

OH, GOODNESS. I'M SORRY.
THERE'S NOTHING **GOOD** ABOUT IT.
THAT'S NOT QUITE WHAT I MEANT, DEAR.

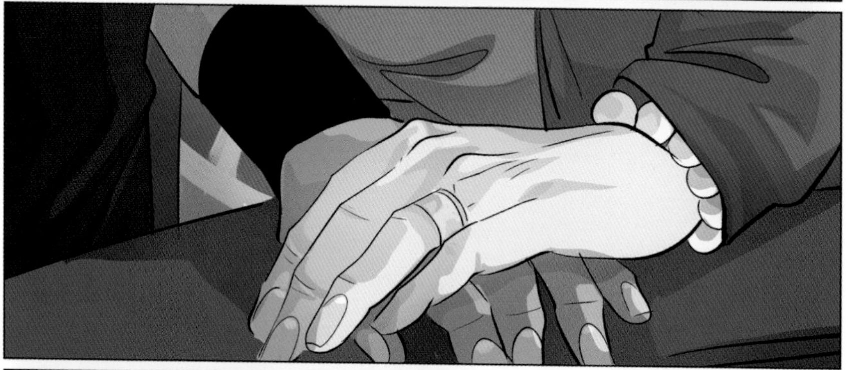

WHEN THEY WERE TAKEN AWAY, I STARTED LISTENING TO LOUD MUSIC. IT'S ALSO WHY I SPEND TIME WITH THOSE "GOONS," LIKE YOU CALLED THEM. I GUESS I JUST DON'T WANT TO LOSE ANYONE ELSE, SO THAT'S WHY I STAY FRIENDS WITH THEM.
I WAS A GOOD KID. I NEVER DID ANYTHING TO BRING NEGATIVE ATTENTION TO MY PARENTS.
MOST EVERYTHING MY PARENTS DID HERE, THEY DID IN FEAR.

I CAN IMAGINE.
MY PARENTS AREN'T BAD PEOPLE. THEY AREN'T CRIMINALS. THEY CAME HERE SO I COULD HAVE A GOOD LIFE.
AND NOW THEY DON'T EVEN GET TO BE HERE FOR IT.
THAT'S WHY YOU LIVE WITH YOUR AUNT? NURSE GINA?
YES.
AND YOU CAN'T VISIT YOUR PARENTS?

NO. I'M A DACA KID, SO I CAN'T LEAVE THE COUNTRY.
COMING BACK INTO THE STATES AFTER VISITING DEPORTEES IS TOO MUCH OF A RISK GOING THROUGH IMMIGRATION, EVEN FOR CITIZENS. SO I DON'T REALLY KNOW IF I'LL EVER SEE THEM AGAIN. IT'S HARD TO UNDERSTAND.

IT'S NOT BEYOND MY DEPTH OF UNDERSTANDING. I'M JEWISH, DARLING.

MY HUSBAND AND I WERE YOUNG WHEN THE NAZI RULE CAME TO AN END. A DECADE LATER, WHEN WE MET, THERE WAS STILL A GREAT DEAL OF ANTI-SEMITIC HATRED AIMED AT US.
EVEN IN SOUTHERN CALIFORNIA.
I'M SO SORRY. HOW DID YOU MEET?

"I WAS NINETEEN."
"I GREW UP IN SAN FRANCISCO, BUT I LOVED MOVIES SO MUCH THAT I ALWAYS WANTED TO LIVE IN LOS ANGELES. IT FELT SO CLOSE, BUT SO DISTANT AT THE SAME TIME."
"MY COUSIN RACHEL WANTED TO LIVE THERE AS WELL, SO ONE DAY, IT MUST HAVE BEEN IN THE SPRING OF '53, I PACKED MY BAGS AND WE HEADED SOUTH TOGETHER."

"I GOT A JOB AS A WAITRESS AT THE PARAMOUNT COMMISSARY."
CAFE CONTINENTAL
"I WAS ON A BREAK FROM WORK ONE AFTERNOON AND EZRA SAW ME OUTSIDE. HE TOOK HIS BREAKS AT THE SAME TIME. HE PASSED ME EVERY DAY FOR A WEEK BEFORE HE BUILT UP THE COURAGE TO SAY HELLO."

WHAT DID HE DO?

HE WORKED ON SET CONSTRUCTION FOR THE PICTURES THERE, SO HE WAS ALWAYS FILTHY.

"I FOUND IT ENDEARING."

"HE BEGAN COURTING ME. I WELCOMED IT. ON OUR FIRST DATE, HE'D CLEANED UP SO WELL IT WAS IMPOSSIBLE FOR ME NOT TO FALL HEAD OVER HEELS."
"THAT'S REALLY SWEET. WHERE DID HE TAKE YOU?"
"WHERE ELSE? THE MOVIES."
"HE KNEW I LOVED THEM, SO AFTER A ROMANTIC DINNER, HE TOOK ME TO SEE THE NEW AUDREY HEPBURN PICTURE. I COULDN'T HAVE ASKED FOR ANYTHING BETTER."
VOGUE
VOGUE
VOGUE

"GOING TO THE MOVIES WASN'T A CASUAL DATE YOU EXPERIENCED IN YOUR PAJAMAS LIKE TODAY. IT WAS AN EVENT. IT WAS SPECIAL. NOTHING SHORT OF REVERENT AND MAGICAL."

YOU SEE, I'D GROWN UP LOVING *NOTORIOUS* AND *ROPE*. INGRID BERGMAN, FARLEY GRANGER.

WHO?

YOU'VE GOT A COMPUTER PHONE IN YOUR POCKET, DON'T YOU? YOU'VE GOT NO EXCUSE, DEAR.
CANDY?

"A LITTLE WHILE INTO OUR COURTSHIP, HE WAS HIRED TO HELP BUILD ONE OF THE LARGEST INDOOR SETS FOR PARAMOUNT PICTURES."
"IT WAS A MONTH-AND-A-HALF JOB, LONG HOURS, SO I REGULARLY BROUGHT HIM HIS DINNER."
"I WAS HAPPY TO. EZRA WAS WORKING WITH FILMMAKERS AND ARTISTS I HAD ADMIRED FOR A LONG TIME, SO I MADE AN EVENT OUT OF THAT, TOO."
"I ALWAYS LOVED CLOTHING AND JEWELRY, AND I REFUSED TO ARRIVE ON A PROPER FILM SET APPEARING ANYTHING LESS THAN GLAMOROUS."

"MY ATTENTION TO FASHION DIDN'T GO UNNOTICED BY MS. EDITH HEAD, WHO WAS THE COSTUME DESIGNER FOR THE PICTURE."
"MEETING HER . . . IT WAS A DREAM."
"I HAPPENED TO HAVE MY SKETCHBOOK WITH ME, AND SHE TOOK A PEEK. SHE COMPLIMENTED MY DRAWINGS AND MY STYLE AND TOLD ME I HAD AN EYE. FOR DESIGN."
"I BEGAN TO STUDY COSTUME AND FASHION IN MY FREE TIME. I CONSUMED IT. MY PASSION FOR IT GREW."
"EVENTUALLY, IT'S WHAT I DEDICATED ALL OF MY TIME TO."

"SOMETIME LATER, MY EZRA BOOKED A LARGE, WELL-PAID CONSTRUCTION JOB OUTSIDE OF THE FILM INDUSTRY."

"IT WAS EXCITING BECAUSE IT MEANT THAT HE WOULD BE GETTING PAID ENOUGH FOR US TO FINALLY BUY A HOME AND HAVE A WEDDING. IT WAS STEADY WORK FOR A FEW YEARS AND REALLY HELPED US START A LIFE TOGETHER . . ."

. . . RIGHT HERE IN SANTA CLARITA.

YOU DON'T MEAN . . .

I MOST CERTAINLY DO.
RIGHT WHERE WE ARE SITTING, YOUNG LADY.
MY HUSBAND HELPED BUILD THIS PLACE.

THAT'S INSANE! ***SERIOUSLY?***

ABSOLUTELY. THIS PLACE IS MORE SPECIAL TO ME THAN YOU COULD EVER IMAGINE.
EZRA AND I SPENT OUR HONEYMOON HERE WHEN THE PARK OPENED IN 1960. GOODNESS ME, HALF A CENTURY AGO.
I HAD NO IDEA. WHAT WAS THIS PLACE LIKE BACK THEN?

"OH, MANY THINGS WERE THE SAME."
"SOME THINGS HAVE SINCE CHANGED A BIT. THE COSTUMES. THAT HORRID DRAGON ROLLER COASTER WAS ADDED A FEW DECADES AGO. BUT THE BONES ARE STILL HERE."
"WHAT MY EZRA BUILT."

"I'D NEVER SEEN HIM HAPPIER."
"HE TOOK SO MUCH PRIDE IN HIS WORK. IT WAS JUST ONE OF THE THINGS I LOVED ABOUT HIM."
"HE ALWAYS SAID THAT THE HATRED HE EXPERIENCED FOR BEING JEWISH, THE NASTY COMMENTS AND WHISPERS, IT ALL WENT AWAY WHEN HE WAS BUILDING. HE WAS ABLE TO TUNE IT ALL OUT."

LIKE YOU DO WITH YOUR MUSIC, I SUPPOSE.

I KNOW TUNING OUT YOUR FEELINGS, NOT DEALING WITH THINGS, ISN'T ALWAYS THE BEST WAY TO GO. I JUST DON'T KNOW WHAT TO DO.
WHAT HAPPENED WITH YOUR PARENTS, IT MIGHT HELP TO WRITE IT ALL DOWN. PUT TO WORDS HOW YOU FEEL.
COMPOSE A SONG. OR WRITE YOUR PARENTS A LETTER. DO YOU KNOW ABOUT LETTER WRITING? THAT'S NOT SOMETHING YOUR GENERATION DOES, IS IT?
I USED TO LOVE WRITING LETTERS.

I CAN WRITE A LETTER. THAT'S NOT A BAD IDEA.
THANKS.
ANYTIME.

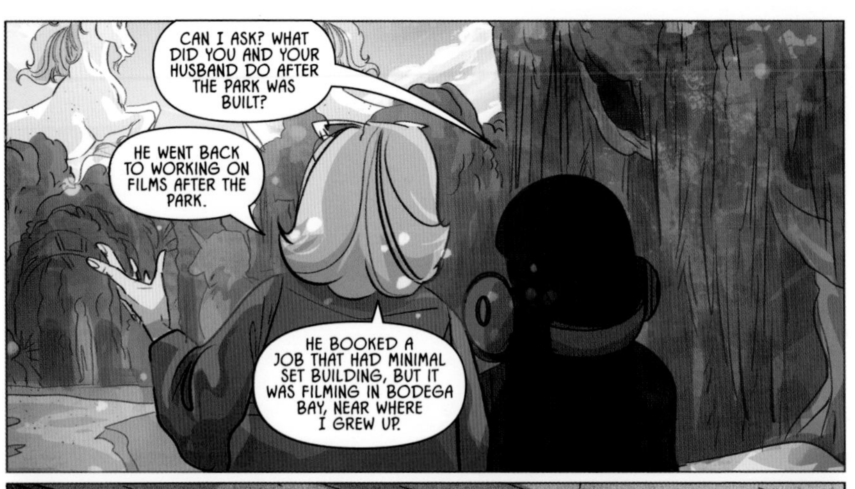

CAN I ASK? WHAT DID YOU AND YOUR HUSBAND DO AFTER THE PARK WAS BUILT?
HE WENT BACK TO WORKING ON FILMS AFTER THE PARK.
HE BOOKED A JOB THAT HAD MINIMAL SET BUILDING, BUT IT WAS FILMING IN BODEGA BAY, NEAR WHERE I GREW UP.

"I VISITED HIM DURING PREPRODUCTION AND RAN INTO MS. HEAD AGAIN. SHE REMEMBERED ME, AND WE SPOKE A BIT ABOUT COSTUMES. HOW SHE WAS A COSTUMER, NOT A DESIGNER. THEY'RE VERY DIFFERENT, YOU KNOW."

"EDITH USED TO SAY, 'IF YOU WANT ANYTHING, YOU WEAR THE RIGHT DRESS.'"

"SHE ASKED ME ABOUT MY AMBITIONS, AND SOMEHOW, I ENDED UP JOINING EZRA ON SET, ASSISTING THE WARDROBE SUPERVISOR MS. RIGGS."

"THAT DAY I WASN'T EVEN WEARING A DRESS, BUT SHE LOVED DESIGNING FOR MEN, AND WHAT I WAS WEARING MUST HAVE SPARKED HER INTEREST."

"THAT'S HOW I BEGAN MY WORK."
"I WORKED IN COSTUME FOR MANY YEARS IN FILM. I LOVED IT SO."
"MANY MEN BACK THEN FOUND THEIR PRIDE SHATTERED IF THEIR WIFE WORKED OR BROUGHT IN MONEY, BUT NOT MY EZRA. HE ALWAYS SAW HOW HAPPY IT MADE ME."
"ALWAYS."

THAT'S REALLY COOL. THAT HE WAS SO SUPPORTIVE, I MEAN.
DID YOU AND HE EVER HAVE KIDS?

NO.

I CAN'T BELIEVE YOUR HUSBAND BUILT THE PLACE THAT MY PARENTS BROUGHT ME TO SO MANY TIMES . . .
AND MANY OTHERS, SWEETHEART. MANY OTHERS.

I WAS ALWAYS HAPPY HERE.
AT KINGDOM ADVENTURE, YOU CAN BE ANYONE OR ANYTHING. IT DOESN'T MATTER. MY PARENTS TOLD ME, "LOOK AT LA PRINCESSA BRIANNA, SHE USED HER BRAIN, SHE ESCAPED AND LIVED HER LIFE. YOU CAN DO IT, TOO."
BUT OUT IN TOWN, EVERYTHING BLENDS INTO ITSELF. THE HOUSES, THE PEOPLE. IT'S LIKE EVERYONE HERE WANTS TO BE THE SAME.

THAT MIGHT BE WHY THEY ENDED UP IN THIS TOWN. TO BLEND IN.
IT'S EXHAUSTING.
WHAT IS?
HIDING.
LIFE IS HARD. IT IS. BUT IF THERE'S ONE THING I CAN TELL YOU . . .
JUST ONE?
YES, YES, I KNOW. I CAN'T HELP IT IF I'M FULL OF GOOD ADVICE.
WHAT IS IT?
EMBRACE ADVERSITY.
WITH EVERYTHING YOU HAVE. IT CAN BE A GREAT TEACHER *IF* YOU EMBRACE IT.
LIFE WILL THROW EVERYTHING IT CAN AT YOU. BUT IF YOU FIGURE OUT HOW TO SOLVE A PROBLEM OR FIX A SITUATION, IT CAN MAKE YOU STRONGER. FORCE YOU TO GROW.

BUT THE THING THAT MAKES IT ALL EASIER? HAVING SOMEONE TO HELP YOU THROUGH IT. TO GROW WITH. WHETHER THAT BE A FAMILY MEMBER OR A BOYFRIEND—

OR A GIRLFRIEND.
OR A GIRLFRIEND, SURE.

I DON'T THINK I HAVE SOMEBODY LIKE THAT.
I THINK YOU MIGHT. DOESN'T ALWAYS NEED TO BE ROMANTIC. SOMETIMES YOU JUST NEED TO LOOK A LITTLE CLOSER.

THAT COMPUTER IN YOUR POCKET. IT WORKS RIGHT NOW?
ARE YOU ASKING IF MY PHONE HAS A SIGNAL? SURE.
LOOK UP *THE SOCIETY GIRLS*. A SONG CALLED "SPCLG."

WOAH, THAT'S LOUD!
SEE? I TOLD YOU, ANY MUSIC CAN BE LOUD.
JUST LISTEN TO THE WORDS.

THANKS, JULIO.
ANYTIME, JACKIE.
The Cinnamon Blade

CAREFUL, OLD MAN. CAREFUL.
ONE DAY YOU'LL BE THIS OLD AND YOU'LL SEE HOW MUCH YOU ENJOY SOMEONE DISHING OUT THE "OLD MAN"S.
OH, PLEASE. I'M GONNA BE FIERCE FOREVER.
PULL UP ON YOUR BUCKLE STRAPS!

HA. "FIERCE"? COMEBACKS? FUNNY LITTLE JABS? THAT'S NOT FIERCE, SON.

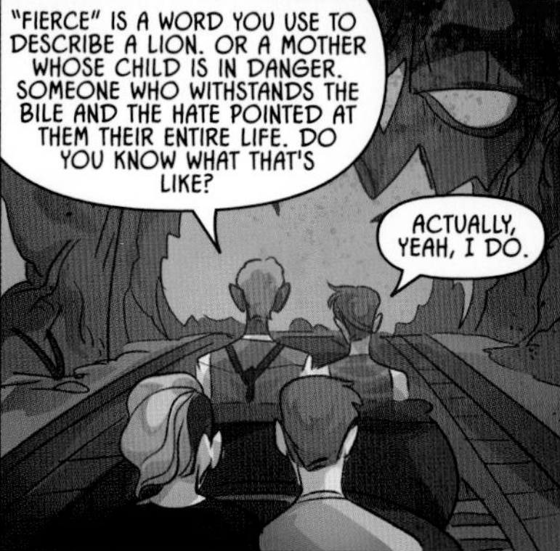
"FIERCE" IS A WORD YOU USE TO DESCRIBE A LION. OR A MOTHER WHOSE CHILD IS IN DANGER. SOMEONE WHO WITHSTANDS THE BILE AND THE HATE POINTED AT THEM THEIR ENTIRE LIFE. DO YOU KNOW WHAT THAT'S LIKE?
ACTUALLY, YEAH, I DO.

I THOUGHT WHEN MY FAMILY MOVED HERE THINGS WOULD GET BETTER. AT MY LAST SCHOOL, BAD STUFF HAPPENED TO ME. I THOUGHT PEOPLE WOULD BE MORE ACCEPTING HERE, BUT SOMETIMES IT FEELS LIKE NIKKI'S MY ONLY FRIEND.

IT'S OKAY TO BE SCARED.

WHEN I WAS YOUR AGE, WHITES AND BLACKS DIDN'T GO TO SCHOOL TOGETHER.
I'M SURE YOU'VE HEARD OF SEPARATE SCHOOLS AND DRINKING FOUNTAINS AND BATHROOMS BEFORE, YES?
YEAH.
THOSE THINGS WERE REAL FOR ME. I HAD THINGS YELLED AT ME, THROWN AT ME. SCARS I WEAR TO THIS DAY.
BEING TOLD YOU'RE DIFFERENT—AND NOT IN A GOOD WAY—IT'S SCARY. IT DOES SOMETHING TO YA.
I DON'T GET WHY PEOPLE CARE SO MUCH.
A LOT OF PEOPLE ARE SCARED OF ANYTHING THAT'S DIFFERENT.
AS FOR YOU, WELL, I'M SURE THOSE BULLIES ARE REACTING TO THE STRENGTH YOU SHOW BY JUST BEING WHO YOU ARE.
THAT'S NICE OF YOU TO SAY.
IT'S NOT ALWAYS AN EASY THING TO DO. IT DOES TAKE COURAGE, THAT'S FOR SURE.
ALL THE STUFF YOU KIDS SAY ABOUT "IT GETS BETTER," WELL, THE WAY THAT HAPPENS IS BY ***MAKING*** IT BETTER. FIGHTING TO MAKE YOURSELF AND OTHERS BETTER. IT'S NOT MAGIC. IT'S BUILDING ON THE HARD WORK OF THOSE WHO CAME BEFORE YOU.
MAKE IT A LITTLE EASIER ON YOURSELF. DON'T ALWAYS DO WHATEVER THAT GIRL TELLS YOU TO. OTHER PEOPLE WILL LIKE YOU JUST FOR BEING YOU.
THANKS, MR. SLOANE.

SO, YOU'RE INTO MRS. ADLER?
PHYLLIS? I SUPPOSE YOU COULD SAY I'M SWEET ON HER.
AND SHE DOESN'T FEEL THE SAME WAY?
UP UNTIL NOW, NO. BESIDES, SHE'S MARRIED.

I THOUGHT HER HUSBAND DIED.
OH, HE DID.
BUT YOU KEEP TRYING ANYWAY?

I KNOW WHEN I'VE PUSHED TOO MUCH. I CAN TELL WHEN SHE WANTS ME GONE.
MOST PEOPLE MY AGE TODAY WOULD SAY THAT YOU SHOULD PROBABLY LEAVE HER ALONE, THEN.
THIS IS THE LAST TIME I'LL LIKELY SAY THIS TO SOMEBODY YOUR AGE, BUT YOU'RE PROBABLY RIGHT.

LONELINESS . . . I'VE SEEN IT JUST DESTROY PEOPLE.
NOBODY SHOULD EVER FEEL LIKE THEY ARE ALONE. AT ANY AGE.

I DON'T THINK EITHER ONE OF THEM DOES ANYMORE.

HELLO, LADIES. SHALL WE?
WHY NOT?

A FEW DAYS LATER . . .
Daniel
Hey, can I get a ride with you today? I want to say hi to Allen.
Sure, but it'll have to be early. I'm playing for the residents today.
No problem.

Here.

HEY, JACKIE. THANKS AGAIN FOR THE RIDE.
HI, JACKIE!

HEY, GUYS!

CAN I COME? PLEASE?
NEXT TIME, 'K? I'LL TAKE YOU SOON. PROMISE.
FINE.

ALL RIGHT. LOVE YOU, BUDDY. I'LL SEE YOU LATER.
LOVE YOU, TOO.

BYE, JACKIE!

BYE, CALEB! SEE YOU SOON!

YOU'RE REALLY SWEET TO HIM.

HE'S HAD A HARD TIME OPENING UP. HE'S BEEN READING A LOT ABOUT KOREA LATELY, AND I WORRY HE FEELS LIKE HE'S NOT PART OF THE FAMILY.

HE COULD JUST BE INTERESTED IN WHERE HE COMES FROM. I THINK A LOT OF PEOPLE ARE.

MAYBE. I'M NOT TOO CONCERNED. HE STARTED OPENING UP MORE AND MORE AFTER WE TOOK HIM TO KINGDOM ADVENTURE.
REALLY?
WELL, YEAH, I MEAN, AFTER YOU HUNG OUT WITH HIM. I THINK HE HAS A CRUSH ON YOU NOW.
THAT'S ADORABLE.

I KNOW WE DITCHED YOU THAT DAY, BUT YOU SHOWED HIM A BUNCH OF STUFF AND THAT MADE HIM FEEL GOOD. LIKE SOMEONE ELSE WAS INTERESTED IN THE SAME THINGS AS HIM.
SO THANKS.
OH. YOU'RE WELCOME.
HE WANTS CHURROS ALL THE TIME NOW, TOO.

WELL, WHO DOESN'T ALWAYS WANT A CHURRO?
TRUE.
YOU USUALLY GET A RIDE WITH NIKKI. THINK SHE'LL BE JEALOUS YOU AREN'T WITH HER?
AT HER BECK AND CALL? MOST LIKELY.

YOU LOOKED IT UP! YOU LEARNED IT! THE SOCIETY GIRLS SONG!
THAT WAS WONDERFUL, DARLING. JUST WONDERFUL!
THANKS, PHYLLIS. IT WAS MY PLEASURE.

HI, ALLEN! HOW ARE YOU?
DOING WELL, SON! NICE TO SEE YOU!
YOU TOO. SEE YOU IN A FEW DAYS FOR YOUR NEXT PARK VISIT!

KINGDOM ADVENTURE, HERE WE COME!

I WANNA EAT BEFORE I FILM ANOTHER VIDEO.
I NEED TO TAKE NOTES ON BRIANNA'S COSTUME AND CHARACTER MOVEMENTS, THEN I'M GONNA RIDE ELDRIC'S SPINE.

OH NO, LOOKS LIKE WE HAVE TO SPLIT OFF AGAIN!

WELL, IF BERKE IS GONNA EAT, THEN I NEED SOMEONE TO RIDE WITH.
COME ON, DANIEL.

PADDLE BOATS?
PADDLE BOATS.

YOU HAVEN'T PULLED THE WOOL OVER MY EYES, YOU KNOW. I'M VERY AWARE OF WHAT YOU'RE DOING.
HUH?
WHAT ARE YOU TALKING ABOUT?

DON'T PATRONIZE ME.
THIS SCHEMING, THIS S.T.O.P. THING YOU AND YOUR FRIENDS HAVE BEEN DOING ALL SUMMER. IT'S VERY OBVIOUS, DEAR. COME ON. OUT WITH IT.

WELL, IF SOMEONE DIES HERE WITH US AND WE GET LIFETIME PASSES, WE THOUGHT IT WOULD JUST SORT OF BE . . . I DON'T KNOW. WE DIDN'T THINK WE'D BE HURTING ANYBODY.
HOW DID YOU FIND OUT?

YOU JUST TOLD ME. I WAS LYING BEFORE, I DIDN'T ACTUALLY KNOW ANY DETAILS. I JUST SUSPECTED YOU WERE UP TO SOMETHING, BUT EXACTLY WHAT, I REALLY WASN'T SURE.
I'M SO SORRY. PLEASE DON'T BE MAD.

MAD? WHAT DO I CARE? THIS IS THE MOST FUN I'VE HAD IN AGES.
WELL, IF YOU KNEW SOMETHING WAS GOING ON, WHY DO YOU WANT TO COME WITH US SO OFTEN? YOU THAT BORED?
BEFORE MY EZRA DIED, HE ASKED TO BE CREMATED. TYPICALLY, THERE IS A POWERFUL TABOO AGAINST CREMATION IN THE JEWISH FAITH, BUT AFTER HIS PARENTS PASSED, AND AS WE GOT OLDER, WE BECAME LESS RELIGIOUS AND PRACTICED MUCH LESS.

WE CAME HERE SO OFTEN WHEN WE WERE YOUNG. HE NEVER SPECIFIED, BUT I KNEW WHERE HE WAS MEANT TO BE. WHERE HE WANTED TO REST.
HE DIDN'T HAVE TO SAY.
WHEN THE PARK OPENED, WE SHARED A SPECIAL MOMENT IN THE UNICORN GLEN. IT WAS THE HAPPIEST I'VE EVER BEEN. THE HAPPIEST HE'D EVER BEEN, TOO.

WAIT A MINUTE. THAT'S WHY YOU TAKE SO LONG AT SECURITY. THAT'S WHY YOU WANT TO GO TO THE GLEN AND SIT SO MUCH.
YOU'RE. . . WHAT'S THE PHRASE? CASING THE JOINT!

BRAVO. NOT MANY PEOPLE KNOW, BUT THEY REMOVE GUESTS FROM THE PREMISES EVERY DAY FOR ATTEMPTING TO SPREAD ASHES IN THE HAUNTED FOREST AND THE UNICORN GLEN. WHEN THAT HAPPENS, THE PARK STAFF SWEEP THEM UP IMMEDIATELY AND DEPOSIT THEM IN THE TRASH.
THAT'S NOT HAPPENING TO MY EZRA.

WOW. I . . . I HAD NO IDEA.
I SUPPOSE WE ALL HAVE OUR REASONS FOR COMING HERE, BUT AT SOME POINT, I THINK WE ALL HAVE TO LET GO.

WHAT DO YOU MEAN?

WELL, DO YOU PLAN ON COMING HERE EVERY WEEK FOR THE REST OF YOUR LIFE? YOU'RE ALMOST DONE WITH SCHOOL. ARE YOU GOING TO STAY HERE IN SANTA CLARITA?
I DON'T KNOW. MY PARENTS WANT ME TO GO TO COLLEGE, BUT WE CAN'T REALLY AFFORD IT.
THERE ARE SCHOLARSHIPS, GRANTS. YOU'RE VERY SMART, JACKIE. TALENTED, TOO.

TALENTED?

YOU PLAYED YOUR GUITAR FOR US TODAY AT THE HOME. YOU CAN ORGANIZE AND PLAN EVENTS VERY WELL FOR SOMEONE SO YOUNG.
YOU SPEAK ENGLISH AND SPANISH.
I'M NOT SURE THAT LAST ONE IS A TALENT. I'VE ALWAYS SPOKEN BOTH.
NOT EVERYONE CAN SPEAK MORE THAN ONE LANGUAGE, THOUGH. HAVING THE ABILITY TO DO THAT MEANS THAT A WHOLE OTHER WORLD OPENS UP FOR YOU.

YOU'VE OBVIOUSLY NEVER SEEN ONE OF THOSE VIDEOS WHERE SOMEONE GETS HARASSED BY SOME SMALL-TOWN, LOWLIFE RACIST WHO CAN'T STAND HEARING SPANISH OR CHINESE OR WHATEVER.
FORGET THOSE PEOPLE.
DO YOU THINK A WELL-PAID LAWYER WHO CAN TRANSLATE FOR LEGAL PROCEEDINGS EVEN THINKS ABOUT THOSE FOOLS? THEY'RE BUSY HELPING PEOPLE WHO NEED IT.
PEOPLE LIKE YOUR PARENTS.

WHAT HAPPENED IN THE UNICORN GLEN? WHY WAS IT SO SPECIAL FOR YOU AND YOUR HUSBAND?
UNICORN HENRY HAS HAD SEVERAL DIFFERENT INCARNATIONS OVER THE YEARS. ON OUR HONEYMOON, EZRA GIFTED ME A LIMITED-EDITION BROOCH OF HENRY. MAJESTIC, BEAUTIFUL.

NOT LIKE THE GOOFY COSTUME CHARACTER THEY HAVE NOW.
IT WAS BEAUTIFUL.

WHAT HAPPENED TO IT?
I LOST IT YEARS AGO. I CRIED FOR AGES.

YOU AREN'T GOING TO TELL MY AUNT WHAT WE'VE BEEN DOING, ARE YOU?
DON'T BE RIDICULOUS. IF I'M GOING TO DIE, I'D RATHER IT BE HERE THAN ANYWHERE ELSE.
AND THEN, AT LEAST YOU GET SOMETHING OUT OF IT.

BESIDES, IF SHE FOUND OUT SHE'D STOP THE PROGRAM, AND THEN I'D LOSE MY RIDE HERE. AND WE CAN'T LET THAT HAPPEN, NOW CAN WE?
THANKS, PHYLLIS. YOU'RE THE BEST.
DON'T MENTION IT.

A FEW DAYS LATER . . .
OH NO. I FORGOT.
IT'S THERAPY DOG DAY. I SCHEDULED THIS LAST WEEK.
HELLO, DEAR. HAND HER TO ME.
WHAT? HOW COME?

MISS CHAVEZ, WE WANTED TO SHOW YOU HOW MUCH WE APPRECIATE THE WORK YOU'VE PUT IN TO MAKE OUR LIVES FUN AND EXCITING AGAIN. IT'S NOT SOMETHING WE WILL FORGET.

I . . . I DON'T KNOW WHAT TO SAY.

WE KNOW A CARD ISN'T MUCH, BUT YOU'VE DONE MORE TO HELP US FEEL LIKE WE'RE NOT COOPED UP THAN ANY OTHER ACTIVITIES PERSON WE'VE HAD.
THAT, AND WE LOVE IT WHEN YOU PLAY THE GUITAR FOR US.

I CAN'T DO THIS ANYMORE.

I'M OUT.

EXCUSE ME? WHAT DO YOU MEAN OUT?
I MEAN IT. I'M DONE.
I DON'T WANT TO DO THIS ANYMORE.

ARE YOU SAYING YOU WANT TO STOP DOING . . . S.T.O.P.?

YES, WHAT WE'RE DOING, IT'S WRONG. I . . . FEEL GROSS.

OH, GET OVER YOURSELF. WE AREN'T DOING ANYTHING BAD.
BESIDES, YOU CAN'T LEAVE. YOU'RE THE ONLY REASON WE HAVE ACCESS TO ALL THOSE SMELLY OLD PEOPLE.

YEAH, WHO AM I SUPPOSED TO GET TO BE IN MY VIDEOS TO MAKE EVERYONE THINK I'M NOT SOME TOTAL SCUMBAG?

MAYBE YOU COULD JUST TRY NOT BEING A TOTAL SCUMBAG.

WHAT DID YOU SAY?
YOU HEARD ME.
I'M GONNA SAY THIS ONCE. YOU'RE NOT CHANGING ANYTHING.
YOU'LL KEEP PICKING UP THOSE OLD FARTS AND WATCHING THEM AT THE PARK OR WE WILL ALL SAY THIS WAS YOUR IDEA-WHICH IT WAS. YOU'D GET IN TROUBLE. YOUR AUNT WOULD LOSE HER JOB.
IT'S IN YOUR BEST INTEREST TO SHUT UP AND JUST DO WHAT WE SAY.
ALL OF YOU? YOU'LL ALL DO THAT?
DANIEL?
WOW.

LATER THAT WEEK . . .

JACKIE?

HEY.

HEY.
HI, CALEB.

GIVE US A MINUTE, 'K, BUDDY?
OKAY.

GO AWAY. I'M MAD AT YOU. YOU SHOULD HAVE BACKED ME UP.
I'M SORRY. REALLY. IT WAS WRONG.
I DON'T KNOW HOW TO SAY NO TO NIKKI. SHE'S BEEN SUCH A GOOD FRIEND TO ME. I DON'T WANT TO LOSE THAT.

I HATE TO BREAK IT TO YOU, DANNY, BUT YOU'RE NOT NIKKI'S FRIEND. YOU'RE HER ACCESSORY.

UH . . . WHAT?

NIKKI WILL WAVE A PRIDE FLAG AROUND BECAUSE IT MAKES HER FEEL GOOD TO HAVE A GAY FRIEND WHO WILL DO WHATEVER SHE WANTS.
THAT'S NOT TRUE.
MEXICANA

WELL, THINK WHAT YOU WANT. BUT I'VE KNOWN HER LONGER THAN YOU HAVE, AND SHE'S NOT A GOOD FRIEND TO YOU. SHE BOSSES YOU AROUND. I WOULD KNOW.

SHE BOSSES YOU AROUND, TOO.
YEAH, SO I CAN SEE HOW I SOUND LIKE A HYPOCRITE, BUT HONESTLY . . .
I THINK I'D RATHER BE HERE WITH THESE PEOPLE THAN WITH NIKKI AND BERKE.
I THINK I CAN SEE WHY.
I SHOULD HAVE BACKED YOU UP. I'M SORRY.
IT'S FINE, DANNY. WE ALL DO THINGS WE AREN'T PROUD OF.

I BROUGHT CALEB SO WE COULD HELP WITH THE MOVIE NIGHT.
HOW DID YOU KNOW WE WERE HAVING MOVIE NIGHT?

I TOLD HIM. WE'VE BEEN TEXTING! HE TAUGHT ME HOW.

HEY, CALEB.
ARE YOU STILL READING THAT BOOK ABOUT KOREAN IMMIGRATION AND SAN FRANCISCO?
THE EARLY 1900S ONE, YEAH.

THIS IS MY FRIEND PHYLLIS. SHE LIVED IN SAN FRANCISCO IN THE THIRTIES AND FORTIES.
HELLO THERE.

REALLY? WOW! WERE THERE LOTS OF KOREANS AND CHINESE PEOPLE? WHAT WAS THEIR CHINATOWN LIKE? WERE THE CABLE CARS TOTALLY DIFFERENT FROM THE WAY THEY ARE NOW?

COME SIT DOWN, YOUNG MAN. YOU'RE GOING TO HURT YOURSELF.

HE'S THRILLED. THANKS FOR THAT.
SURE. PHYLLIS HAS LIVED A VERY INTERESTING LIFE.
YOU KNOW SHE MADE COSTUMES FOR MOVIES? AND HER HUSBAND BUILT KINGDOM ADVENTURE?

SERIOUSLY?
YEAH. SHE'S AWESOME. I WISH THERE WERE SOMETHING NICE I COULD DO FOR HER.
CONSIDERING.
YOU MEAN, LIKE, A GIFT?

YEAH, THERE WAS THIS UNICORN HENRY BROOCH THAT HER HUSBAND GOT HER WHEN THE PARK OPENED BUT SHE LOST IT. IT'S RARE AND–
WAS IT THIS ONE?

HOW DID YOU FIND THAT SO FAST?
I JUST SEARCHED ONLINE. THIS ONE'S GOT A FEW MISSING JEWELS, SO IT'S NOT EXPENSIVE. I'M JUST GONNA GET IT.

THANKS, DANNY.
YOU KEEP CALLING ME THAT.
I KNOW.

HOLA, AMOR.
HEY, TÍA.

JACKIE, THIS IS SO WONDERFUL. WHAT YOU'RE DOING HERE, IT'S GOOD.
MEXICANA

"THE RESIDENTS ARE HAPPY."

"THEY HAVE NEW FRIENDS."

"THEIR MENTAL AND EMOTIONAL HEALTH IS IMPROVING."
"IT'S EVEN GIVEN SOME OF THEM MORE ENERGY."

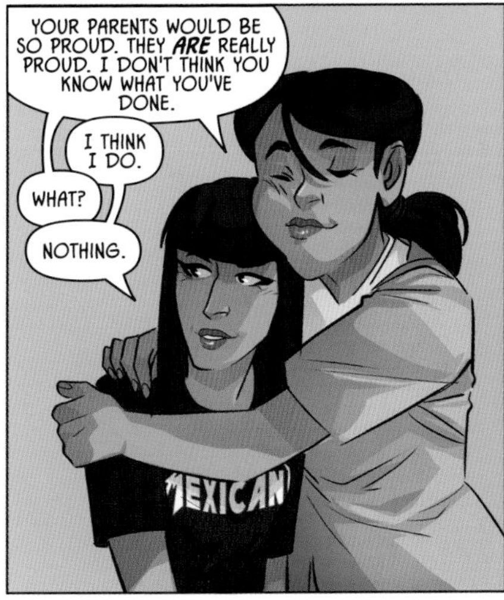
YOUR PARENTS WOULD BE SO PROUD. THEY *ARE* REALLY PROUD. I DON'T THINK YOU KNOW WHAT YOU'VE DONE.
I THINK I DO.
WHAT?
NOTHING.

GO, ENJOY THE MOVIE.

CAW
CAW
CAW

I WORKED ON THIS FILM, YOU KNOW.
WE KNOW, PHYLLIS! WE KNOW.

THAT'S WHY I CHOSE IT.

TIPPI'S GREEN SUIT IS PERFECTION. YOU SEE, EDITH INSISTED ON SIMPLICITY THERE, KNOWING IT WOULD AGE WELL.

THERE'S VERY LITTLE TO DATE IT. SIX DIFFERENT COPIES OF THAT COSTUME WERE MADE.

OH, I DO LOVE ETHEL'S COAT THERE.
THIS IS MY FAVORITE SCENE.

HOW COME?

JUST WATCH, JUST WATCH.

"THIS IS A WONDERFUL SCENE WHERE THE CHARACTERS ATTEMPT TO FIGURE OUT WHAT'S HAPPENING WITH THE BIRDS, BUT THEY DON'T EVER FIGURE IT OUT."

BEST SCENE IN THE FILM.

AAAAAAH! SPOILERS!

THIS MOVIE IS SO OLD, DANNY. YOU DON'T GET TO BE UPSET ABOUT SPOILERS.

YOU MEAN THEY NEVER EXPLAIN IT? WHY?

WELL, THAT'S NOT THE POINT, YOU SEE.
TO EXPLAIN AND GIVE IT SOME REASON WOULD MAKE IT A SCIENCE-FICTION PICTURE. THE TENSION COMES FROM KNOWING SOMETHING ISN'T RIGHT BUT NOT KNOWING WHAT TO DO.

IN *REAR WINDOW*, MR. STEWART SAYS: "SOMETIMES IT'S WORSE TO STAY THAN IT IS TO RUN." AND THAT'S IT.
THESE CHARACTERS DON'T KNOW YET THAT THE BEST SOLUTION TO THEIR PROBLEM IS TO STOP ANALYZING IT AND SIMPLY GET OUT.

I CAN'T BELIEVE HOW MANY TIMES WE'VE GONE TO THE PARK THIS SUMMER.
I KNOW. IT'S BEEN A LOT OF FUN.
NIKKI IS NOT GOING TO BE HAPPY WE'RE HANGING OUT SO MUCH.

I DON'T CARE. REALLY.

ALLEN ISN'T ANSWERING ANY OF MY MESSAGES. I TOLD HIM NOT TO FORGET TO CHARGE HIS PHONE.
EXICANA

OH, JACKIE. DANIEL.
HI, TÍA.

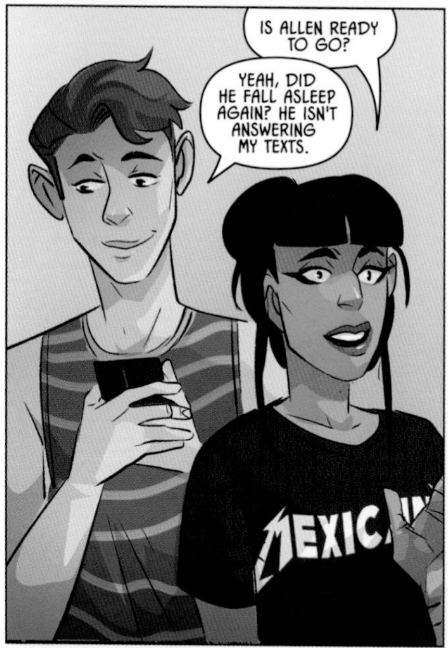
IS ALLEN READY TO GO?
YEAH, DID HE FALL ASLEEP AGAIN? HE ISN'T ANSWERING MY TEXTS.

I'M . . . I'M SO SORRY.
ALLEN PASSED AWAY IN HIS SLEEP LAST NIGHT.

NO.
WHAT?

HE WENT PEACEFULLY. HE WASN'T IN ANY PAIN. IT'S . . .
IT'S THE BEST ANY OF US CAN HOPE FOR.

I SUPPOSE THAT'S A WRAP ON THE FLIRTING.

IS THAT REALLY ALL YOU CARE ABOUT?

I CAN'T BELIEVE IT. NO . . .

I DON'T MEAN TO APPEAR COLD, BUT HE LIVED A GOOD LIFE. HE WAS CARED FOR WELL HERE. HIS FAMILY VISITED HIM OFTEN.

WELL, YOU ***DO*** SOUND COLD. YOU DON'T SOUND LIKE YOU CARE THAT HE'S GONE AT ALL.

HOW CAN YOU BE LIKE THIS?
I'VE SEEN MORE THAN MY FAIR SHARE OF PEOPLE COMING IN AND GOING OUT.
ALL RIGHT. EVERYONE NEEDS TO BREATHE. DRINK SOME WATER. TAKE A MINUTE AND CALM DOWN.

I'M PERFECTLY CALM.

WE CAN'T SEEM TO LOCATE HIS CANE. IF ANY OF YOU SEE IT, PLEASE LET ME OR ONE OF THE OTHER NURSES KNOW.

I CAN DRIVE YOU HOME. DO YOU WANT TO GO?

NO . . . I'LL HELP LOOK FOR HIS CANE.

I'LL HELP YOU. FIRST, COME SIT WITH ME FOR A MINUTE. CATCH YOUR BREATH.
JACKIE, I COULD USE YOUR HELP FOR A BIT.

THANKS FOR HELPING.
THIS IS JUST LIKE BEFORE. IT'S FAST, BUT HIS FAMILY IS GOING TO COME COLLECT HIS THINGS, AND WE HAVE ANOTHER RESIDENT MOVING IN, SO WE NEED THE ROOM.
SURE.

I DON'T UNDERSTAND. I REALLY DON'T.
WHAT'S THAT? WHY HE DIED?

NO, I JUST . . . WE WOULD NEVER DO THIS. WE WOULD NEVER PUT OUR PARENTS OR OUR ABUELOS OR ABUELAS IN A PLACE LIKE THIS. WE WOULDN'T SEPARATE OURSELVES FROM OUR FAMILY.

NO, WE WOULDN'T. BUT THAT'S LARGELY CULTURAL. IT'S NOT FOR US TO JUDGE.

HELEN, FOR EXAMPLE. SHE DOESN'T HAVE ANY FAMILY LEFT. SHE NEVER HAD ANY KIDS, AND HER WIFE DIED FIVE YEARS AGO. SHE HAS NOWHERE ELSE TO GO.
GEORGE NEEDS CONSTANT CARE BECAUSE OF HIS MEDICAL CONDITIONS.

I'M ABLE TO DO MY JOB AND PROVIDE FOR US BECAUSE THERE ARE PEOPLE WHO NEED HELP.
THIS PLACE SERVES A PURPOSE. WITHOUT IT, A LOT OF PEOPLE WOULDN'T HAVE WHAT THEY NEED. SOME PEOPLE FORM FRIENDSHIPS HERE. FAMILIES.
CRUSHES.

ELDER-CARE FACILITIES GET A BAD RAP, BUT WHEN WE HAVE PEOPLE WHO CARE ABOUT THE RESIDENTS, LIKE YOU DO, IT MAKES THE TIME THEY DO HAVE LEFT HAPPIER, BETTER.
I CAN SEE THAT NOW.

A WEEK LATER . . .

YOU GUYS! MY CHANNEL ISN'T SUSPENDED ANYMORE, SO I'M GONNA GET THE LAST BIT OF FOOTAGE FOR MY NEW VIDEO!
NIKKI'S GONNA FILM FROM THE GROUND TO GET SOME GOOD ESTABLISHING SHOTS . . .
BEAST

AND I SNUCK THIS IN SO I CAN GET SOME SWEET SHOTS WHILE THE COASTER'S GOING.

THIS . . . THIS IS SO STUPID.

OH PLEASE, JACKIE, SHUT UP.
IF YOU'D SCHEDULED THINGS BETTER THAT OLD GUY MIGHT'VE KICKED THE BUCKET HERE AND WE'D ALL HAVE OUR PASSES BY NOW.
NO KIDDING.

WHAT THE—!

WHAT DID YOU JUST SAY?
BEAST

BACK OFF, YOU OLD BAG!

NO, ***YOU*** BACK OFF! OTHERWISE YOUVID GETS TO KNOW THE ***REAL*** YOU AGAIN. I'M ***FILMING*** RIGHT NOW, AND I HAVE NO PROBLEM SENDING THIS TO YOUR CHANNEL'S SPONSOR.
NOT A SINGLE ONE.

THAT'S BERKE BRIDGETOWER FROM YOUVID!
I HEARD HE'S A TOTAL DICK.
WHAT'S HAPPENING?

REMEMBER WHAT WE TALKED ABOUT, JACKIE.
WE'VE GOT STUFF ON YOU, TOO.

SHUT UP, NIKKI. GET A LIFE. REALLY.

WHAT? DANIEL!
YOU HEARD BERKE! IF YOU PUSH HIM HE'S GOING TO GO STRAIGHT TO THAT SMELLY OLD FOLK'S HOME AND TELL WHOEVER IS IN CHARGE EVERYTHING!

YOUNG LADY, WHO DO YOU THINK HE'S GOING TO BELIEVE? A RESIDENT AND HIS ACTIVITIES COORDINATOR OR AN ANGRY TEENAGER HE'S NEVER MET THAT'S SO ADDICTED TO CAFFEINATED SLUDGE IT'S AFFECTED HIS SENSIBILITIES?
RUN ALONG NOW.
MEXICANA
NIKKI, YOUR PHONE. GET SOME GOOD SHOTS. THERE'S NO LINE, SO I'M RIDING THE COASTER. WE'LL DEAL WITH THIS LATER.
DANIEL, WHY ARE YOU DOING THIS? WE'RE SUPPOSED TO BE FRIENDS. WE'RE SUPPOSED TO DO THIS TOGETHER, AUDITION TOGETHER.
THAT'S WHAT *YOU* WANT, NIKKI. I THOUGHT I WANTED THAT, TOO.
BUT I DON'T.

OH, SO, WHAT? YOU'D RATHER HANG OUT WITH OLD PEOPLE AND . . . AND **HER**?
HONESTLY, YEAH.

FINE. I'LL BECOME BRIANNA WITHOUT YOU! YOU TWO DESERVE EACH OTHER!

I THINK WE DO.
THIS **NEED** TO BE WORSHIPPED, NIKKI . . . IT'S NOT HEALTHY.

THIS PARK IS AMAZING, YOUNG LADY, BUT TAKE A LESSON FROM SOMEONE WHO'S BEEN HERE MORE TIMES THAN YOU. IT'S NOT ALL THERE IS TO LIFE.

GASP
OH MY GOD!
LOOK!
NO!

WHAT?
WHAT'S HAPPENING?
HOLY-!
OH MY GOD!
NOOOO!
AAAAAAHHHHHH!
HELP! SOMEBODY HELP!

Querido Papá y Mamá,
A new friend of mine suggested I write a letter to you. I know Tia Gina told you a little bit about what happened this summer.
I'll never forget the sight of Berke falling through the sky, his twisted body on the pavement in front of us.

I HAVE AN IDEA.

BUT IT REQUIRES YOUR HELP.

ANYTHING.

He didn't die, though, in case you're wondering.
They tried to keep it quiet, but everyone's so plugged in nowadays. It was all over the Internet for a bit, then Kingdom Adventure's lawyers swooped in and scrubbed it as best they could.

His selfie stick got caught in his harness and right when the coaster took off, he flew out of it.
Nikki's traumatized.

Understandably so.

WHAT ARE YOU DOING HERE?

WE JUST CAME TO SEE IF YOU'RE OKAY. IF THERE'S ANYTHING YOU NEED.
HAVE YOU EATEN ANYTHING?

WHY? WHAT DO YOU CARE?

JUST LET US KNOW . . . IF YOU NEED SOMETHING, OKAY?

YOU KNOW THEY GAVE US LIFETIME PASSES ANYWAY?
WHAT?

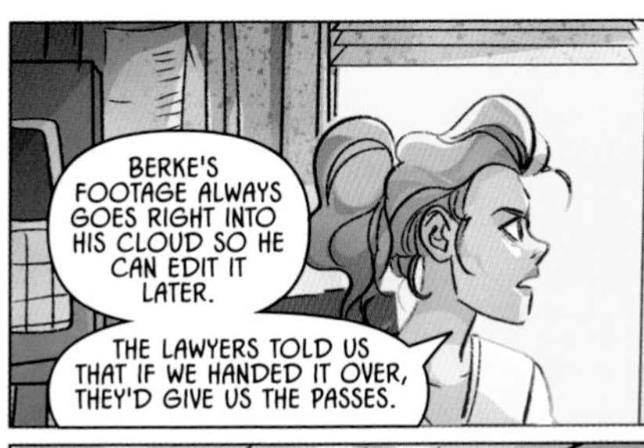
BERKE'S FOOTAGE ALWAYS GOES RIGHT INTO HIS CLOUD SO HE CAN EDIT IT LATER.
THE LAWYERS TOLD US THAT IF WE HANDED IT OVER, THEY'D GIVE US THE PASSES.

THEY SAID WHAT HAPPENED WAS HIS FAULT, BUT THAT THEY WANTED US TO HAVE THEM "FOR OUR TROUBLE."

WHY WOULD I EVER GO BACK THERE? THEY THINK I WANT TO BE THERE AND THINK ABOUT WHAT HAPPENED?
ALL OF THE ATTENTION HE NEEDED . . . *WE* NEEDED, IT'S LIKE THIS IS THE PUNISHMENT FOR WANTING TO BE SEEN. FOR DOING THIS . . . BAD THING.
BESIDES, IT'S NOT LIKE I HAVE FRIENDS TO GO WITH NOW ANYWAY.

TAKE THE PASSES. YOU CAN HAVE THEM FOR ALL I CARE.

NIKKI, WE CAN'T DO THAT. IT'S NOT RIGHT.
AREN'T THEY IN YOUR NAME?
I'LL TAKE CARE OF IT.

And she did.
She signed an agreement with Kingdom Adventure's lawyers promising not to speak about what happened.
BINGO

In exchange, she asked that the passes she and Berke received be put in someone else's name to be used however they saw fit.

HEY, JACK! DID YOU DO IT?
I DID.
WHERE'S MRS. ADLER?

LET'S TAKE THE WHOLE DAY, SHALL WE?
She had them put in the name of Valley Care Living.

That way, family and friends of the residents can take their elderly loved ones to the park for free whenever they want.
TIME TO LIVE DANGEROUSLY.
ALL RIGHT. WE'LL GO BE THE LOOKOUTS. IF ANY STAFF COME BY, WE'LL DISTRACT THEM.
THANK YOU, DANIEL.

RRRRRIIP

READY?
READY.

I miss you both so much.

PHYLLIS, WE HAVE SOMETHING FOR YOU.
YOU DO?

It hurts more than I can describe that you aren't here with me. That I might never see you again.
IT'S NOT NEW, OBVIOUSLY, AND IT'S A LITTLE WORN, BUT . . .

IT'S . . . MY BROOCH. MY UNICORN BROOCH.

THANK YOU. THANK YOU SO MUCH.

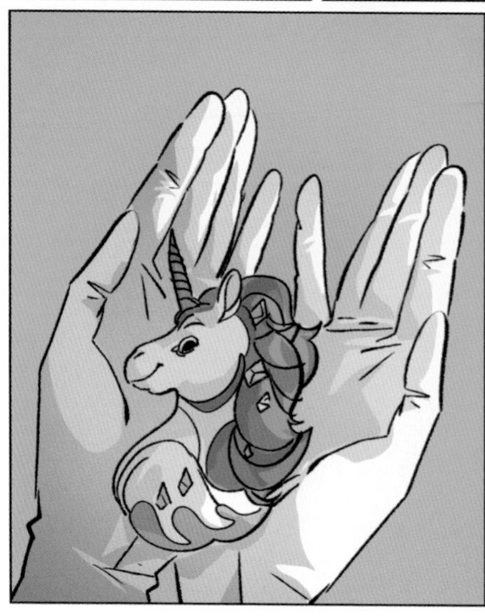

But you came here for me. So I could have a good life. So that life wouldn't pass me by.

So that's what I'll do.
I'll make it count.

I'll do it for you.
I'll do it for me.
And maybe in some strange way, what happened won't hurt as much.
Only time will tell.
Because if this summer has taught me anything . . .

. . . it's that the most important thing in this world . . .
. . . is our time.

ACKNOWLEDGMENTS

For Scott, who believed in me, believed in this idea, and told me it was good. A lifetime together isn't long enough.

I also need to thank Carrie. Your friendship and love are what inspired this book, and considering it was the first idea I had for a graphic novel, I feel like I owe you. Thank you. Also, to Ryan and Justin, who helped me sort out the story when I got stuck. You reminded me that sometimes just standing up for yourself is enough of a resolution. Thank you to Ben, Lindsey, and Gabe. I love you. Thanks for always supporting me and believing in me. To Natalie, for your advice and constant inspiration. Katie, you've helped me with my career more than you know.

Daniel, thanks for always letting me bounce ideas off of you. Your support means everything to me, and you and your work are a constant inspiration.

Thanks to my mom and dad, who always seemed interested in this idea and listened to me talk about it.

This book wouldn't be possible without *mi hermana Mexicana*, my creative partner, Claudia. I am in awe of you and feel so lucky to have found you and to be working with you.

To my agent, Kate, thank you for putting up with me, my million questions, and the hundreds of projects I want to do. Thank you Mariko and Charlotte for helping this book come to life, and thank you to my puppy, Alfie, for hanging out with me while I work. Lastly, thank you, Scott. You encouraged me so much to make this book. I love you, and you're the best.

—Terry Blas

I want to thank everyone who made this book possible.

Terry, who I love as a brother, and we get to do comic books together, which is the coolest thing siblings can do. To Mariko and Charlotte for their dedication and their hard work on making this wonderful adventure come true in print. To Kate, my agent, for her wonderful advice and guidance.

And last but not least, to my wonderful partner, Diana; without you I'd be a headless chicken running around. Thank you so much.

—Claudia Aguirre

SURELY publishes LGBTQIA+ stories by LGBTQIA+ creators, with a focus on new stories, new voices, and untold histories, in works that span fiction and nonfiction, including memoir, horror, comedy, and fantasy. Surely aims to publish books that lend context and perspective to our current struggles and victories, and to support those creators underrepresented in the current publishing world. We are bold, brave, loud, unexpected, daring, unique.

SURELY Curator: Mariko Tamaki
Editor: Charlotte Greenbaum
Designer: Kay Petronio
Managing Editors: Mary O'Mara and Marie Oishi
Production Manager: Alison Gervais
Lettering: Dave Sharpe

Library of Congress Control Number for the hardcover edition 2021930589

Hardcover ISBN 978-1-4197-4666-6
Paperback ISBN 978-1-4197-4667-3

Printed and bound in China

10 9 8 7 6 5 4 3 2 1

ABRAMS The Art of Books
195 Broadway, New York, NY 10007
abramsbooks.com